A Moment of Magic...

"But...you will be safe?" Hermia said almost beneath her breath.

"I will be safe," the Marquis repeated, "because you have saved me."

He looked down at her, and as she stared up at him in the moonlight, his lips came down on hers.

For a moment she could hardly believe what was happening. She felt his mouth take possession of hers and she knew it was what she had yearned for, prayed for. She surrendered herself to him, heart and soul...

A WITCH'S SPELL

A Camfield Novel of Love

Camfield Place,
Hatfield
Hertfordshire,
England

Dearest Reader,

Camfield Novels of Love mark a very exciting era of my books with Jove. They already have nearly two hundred of my books which they have had ever since they became my first publisher in America. Now all my original paperback romances in the future will be published by them.

As you already know, Camfield Place in Hertfordshire is my home, which originally existed in 1275, but was rebuilt in 1867 by the grandfather of Beatrix Potter.

It was here in this lovely house, with the best view of the county, that she wrote *The Tale of Peter Rabbit*. Mr. McGregor's garden is exactly as she described it. The door in the wall that the fat little rabbit could not squeeze underneath and the goldfish pool where the white cat sat twitching its tail are still there.

I had Camfield Place blessed when I came here in 1950 and was so happy with my husband until he died, and now with my children and grandchildren, that I know the atmosphere is filled with love and we have all been very lucky.

It is easy here to write of love and I know you will enjoy the Camfield Novels of Love. Their plots are definitely exciting and the covers very romantic. They come to you, like all my books, with love.

Bless you,

Barbara Cartland

Books by Barbara Cartland

THE ADVENTURER
AGAIN THIS RAPTURE
ARMOUR AGAINST LOVE·
THE AUDACIOUS ADVENTURESS
BARBARA CARTLAND'S BOOK OF BEAUTY AND HEALTH
THE BITTER WINDS OF LOVE
BLUE HEATHER
BROKEN BARRIERS
THE CAPTIVE HEART
THE COIN OF LOVE
THE COMPLACENT WIFE
COUNT THE STARS
CUPID RIDES PILLION
DANCE ON MY HEART
DESIRE OF THE HEART
DESPERATE DEFIANCE
THE DREAM WITHIN
A DUEL OF HEARTS
ELIZABETH EMPRESS OF AUSTRIA
ELIZABETHAN LOVER
THE ENCHANTED MOMENT
THE ENCHANTED WALTZ
THE ENCHANTING EVIL
ESCAPE FROM PASSION
FOR ALL ETERNITY
A GHOST IN MONTE CARLO
THE GOLDEN GONDOLA
A HALO FOR THE DEVIL
A HAZARD OF HEARTS
A HEART IS BROKEN
THE HEART OF THE CLAN
THE HIDDEN EVIL
THE HIDDEN HEART
THE HORIZONS OF LOVE
AN INNOCENT IN MAYFAIR

IN THE ARMS OF LOVE
THE IRRESISTIBLE BUCK
JOSEPHINE EMPRESS OF FRANCE
THE KISS OF PARIS
THE KISS OF THE DEVIL
A KISS OF SILK
THE KNAVE OF HEARTS
THE LEAPING FLAME
A LIGHT TO THE HEART
LIGHTS OF LOVE
THE LITTLE PRETENDER
LOST ENCHANTMENT
LOST LOVE
LOVE AND LINDA
LOVE AT FORTY
LOVE FORBIDDEN
LOVE HOLDS THE CARDS
LOVE IN HIDING
LOVE IN PITY
LOVE IS AN EAGLE
LOVE IS CONTRABAND
LOVE IS DANGEROUS
LOVE IS MINE
LOVE IS THE ENEMY
LOVE ME FOREVER
LOVE ON THE RUN
LOVE TO THE RESCUE
LOVE UNDER FIRE
THE MAGIC OF HONEY
MESSENGER OF LOVE
METTERNICH: THE PASSIONATE DIPLOMAT
MONEY, MAGIC AND MARRIAGE
NO HEART IS FREE
THE ODIOUS DUKE
OPEN WINGS
OUT OF REACH
THE PASSIONATE PILGRIM
THE PRETTY HORSEBREAKERS
THE PRICE IS LOVE

A RAINBOW TO HEAVEN
THE RELUCTANT BRIDE
THE RUNAWAY HEART
THE SCANDALOUS LIFE OF KING CAROL
THE SECRET FEAR
THE SMUGGLED HEART
A SONG OF LOVE
STARS IN MY HEART
STOLEN HALO
SWEET ADVENTURE
SWEET ENCHANTRESS
SWEET PUNISHMENT
THEFT OF A HEART
THE THIEF OF LOVE
THIS TIME IT'S LOVE
TOUCH A STAR
TOWARDS THE STARS
THE UNKNOWN HEART
THE UNPREDICTABLE BRIDE
A VIRGIN IN PARIS
WE DANCED ALL NIGHT
WHERE IS LOVE?
THE WINGS OF ECSTASY
THE WINGS OF LOVE
WINGS ON MY HEART
WOMAN—THE ENIGMA

CAMFIELD NOVELS OF LOVE

THE POOR GOVERNESS
WINGED VICTORY
LUCKY IN LOVE
LOVE AND THE MARQUIS
A MIRACLE IN MUSIC
LIGHT OF THE GODS
BRIDE TO A BRIGAND
LOVE COMES WEST
A WITCH'S SPELL

A NEW CAMFIELD NOVEL OF LOVE BY

BARBARA CARTLAND

A Witch's Spell

A JOVE BOOK

A WITCH'S SPELL

A Jove Book / published by arrangement with
the author

PRINTING HISTORY
Jove edition / May 1984

ISBN: 0-515-07602-3

Jove books are published by The Berkley Publishing Group,
200 Madison Avenue, New York, N.Y. 10016.
The words "A JOVE BOOK" and the "J" with sunburst
are trademarks belonging to Jove Publications, Inc.

PRINTED IN THE UNITED STATES OF AMERICA

Author's Note

The belief in Witchcraft is still very strong today and practised in parts of England and Europe. There are two types of witchcraft—Black and White. White Witches usually use herbs to cure wounds, sores and diseases.

Ten years ago a White Witch from a coven in the North of England was asked:

"Does a Witch possess what others would regard as 'supernatural' powers?"

The answer was:

"A Witch possesses nothing which is not basic in everyone. People in becoming 'civilized' have lost sight of these powers. A Witch cultivates them, learns how to bring them back into use—how to control them and make the power work."

The terrible cruelty of the Witchhunts in England between 1542 and 1684 resulted in a thousand Witches being executed. In Scotland the number executed was higher and death was by burning. In Europe from the fifteenth to the eighteenth century over two hundred thousand Witches died at the stake.

In England in 1736 the statute was repealed and the law no longer punished Witches. By the end of the century the mania for Witchhunts in Europe had disappeared. In rural districts, however, Witches are still revered or feared.

chapter one

1818

COMING from the farm with a basket of eggs on her arm Hermia was humming a little tune at the same time as she was telling herself a story.

Because she was so much alone she invariably enlivened her daily tasks by pretending she was the wife of an Eastern Potentate, or the daughter of an explorer seeking treasures hidden by the Aztecs, or a pearl diver.

Just as she reached the end of the narrow lane which led to Honeysuckle Farm, and was about to join the road which would take her to the village, she heard a man's voice exclaim in a tone of exasperation:

"Damn!"

Hermia started because she had seldom heard a man swear. The country people were God-fearing and soft spoken.

Curious, she hurried down the last few yards of

the lane to have her first sight of an extremely well-bred horse.

She appreciated its appearance and saw that its rider was bending down to pick up its offside hind leg.

She realised that he was looking at the horse's hoof and guessed that it had lost a shoe.

It was something that frequently happened in the neighbourhood because the roads were so rough, and Hermia suspected that the local Blacksmith was not as skilled as his predecessor.

It flashed through her mind however that she did not recognise the horse or its owner, who at the moment had his back to her.

She, however, walked forward to ask in her soft voice:

"Can I help you?"

The Gentleman bending over the horse's hoof did not turn his head.

"Not unless you have something with which to lever a shoe from a hoof!" he replied.

He spoke in an obviously irritated manner, but with the drawl which her brother had told Hermia was fashionable amongst the Bucks in London, and was affected by the aristocratic visitors who stayed with her Uncle, the Earl of Millbrooke, at the Hall.

She guessed this was where the Gentleman whose face she could not see had come from.

Moving closer she realised that what was upsetting him was that the shoe on his horse's hoof had come loose, but was still attached by one nail which he could not dislodge.

This was an accident which had often happened to the horses her brother Peter rode when he was at home.

Without saying anything she put down her basket

and looked at the rough surface of the road. A second later she saw what she sought.

It was a large flat stone and picking it up she moved to the side of the Gentleman who was still struggling to wrench the shoe loose and said:

"Let me try."

He did not glance up at her but merely held his horse's foreleg as he was doing already, and waited while she bent down, slipped the flat stone under the shoe and levered it free from the hoof.

It took a certain amount of strength, but because she was doing it the right way and with a deft movement of her wrist, the shoe was detached from the hoof and clattered onto the road, taking the nail with it.

The Gentleman beside her put the horse's leg down, straightened himself, and said:

"I am extremely grateful to you, and now kindly tell me where I can find a Blacksmith."

He picked the shoe up from the ground as he spoke.

Then for the first time he looked to see who had been skilful enough to help him.

Not realising she was doing so, Hermia, as she bent down to insert the stone under the shoe, had pushed back her sun-bonnet so that, still tied by its ribbons under her chin, it hung down her back.

Her hair could now be seen curling unfashionably over her head in a natural and very attractive manner, and was in the sunshine turned to burning gold.

It was the vivid gold of the daffodils in spring, the jasmine when it first appears after the cold of the winter, and the corn when it is just beginning to ripen in the fields.

Anybody who saw Hermia looked at her hair as if

they did not believe it could possibly be natural, but must owe its vivid colour to the dye-pot.

It complemented the pink-and-white clarity of her skin and the blue of her eyes, which strangely enough were the vivid blue of an alpine flower rather than the soft blue of an English summer sky.

Despite the cynical expression on his face, there was a look of astonishment in the eyes of the Gentleman.

At the same time, if he were surprised by her, Hermia was certainly surprised by him.

Never had she seen a man who looked so sardonic.

His hair was dark, his features clear-cut, and while his eye-brows seemed almost to meet across the bridge of his nose, there was a bored, almost contemptuous expression in his eyes as if he despised everything and everybody.

They stood looking at each other until the Gentleman said dryly:

"You certainly make me believe that the stories of pretty milk-maids are after all, not exaggerated!"

There was a faint twist to his lips which one could hardly call a smile as he added:

"And of course it is an added bonus that you should be intelligent as well!"

As he spoke he drew something from his waistcoat pocket and put it into Hermia's hand, saying:

"Here is something to add to your bottom drawer when you find a hefty young farmer to make you happy."

Then as Hermia would have looked down at what he had given her, he moved a step forward and putting his hand under her chin turned her face up to his.

Before she realised what was happening, before she had time to think, he bent his head and his lips were on hers.

She felt as if he held her prisoner and it was impossible to move or breathe.

Then, as at the back of her mind she knew she must struggle, and at the same time tell him that he insulted her, he released her and with the lithe grace of an athletic man, sprang into the saddle.

While she was still staring at him in bewilderment he said:

"What is more, he will be a very lucky man. Tell him I said so."

He rode off and as Hermia watched the dust from his horse's hoofs rising behind him she thought she must be dreaming.

Only when the stranger was out of sight did she ask herself how she could have been so stupid as to have stood there gaping at him like any half-witted yokel while he kissed her.

It was the first time she had ever been kissed.

Then as she stared down at what she held in her hand, she saw it was a golden guinea, and could hardly believe it was real.

Hermia was used to walking about the countryside by herself and everybody in the village knew her.

It had never struck her for one moment that a stranger might think it odd or as she realised now, mistake her, because of the way she was dressed, for a milk-maid.

Her worn cotton gown was a little too tight from so many washes and her sun-bonnet was faded because she had worn it since she was a child.

Even so she did not look in the least like Molly, the farmer's daughter who helped him to milk his cows.

Nor did she resemble in any way, the middle-aged women who had worked on Honeysuckle Farm, some of them for twenty years.

"A milk-maid!" she whispered to herself, and thought how angry her father would be at what had happened.

Then she could not help thinking it was her own fault.

She had gone to the assistance of the stranger without explaining who she was.

Although he might have guessed from the few words she spoke to him that she was educated, she could hardly blame him for believing her to come from a very different background.

At the same time she thought it was an insult even for a milk-maid to be kissed by a strange man for no reason except that she had helped him.

Because she was not only angry, but in fact humiliated, Hermia's instinct was to throw away the guinea the stranger had given her and hope nobody would ever know what had happened.

Then she told herself that would be a wicked waste of money, for a guinea would buy many of the things which her father paid for himself for the poor and sick in the village.

Times were hard since the war, and it was difficult for the younger men to find employment.

Those who were not fortunate enough to work at the Hall or on the Earl's estate had to feed themselves by growing vegetables and keeping a few chickens.

Hermia looked down again at the guinea and thought

that, if she slipped it into the poor-box at the Church which usually contained nothing, her father would be delighted. He would bless the unknown benefactor, which was very far from her own feelings towards him!

As the full realisation that she had been kissed by a man she had never met before and would never meet again swept over her, Hermia said beneath her breath:

"How dare he! How dare he behave to me in such a manner? It is monstrous that no girl should be safe in a country lane from men like him!"

In the violence of her indignation, her fingers tightened on the guinea and she asked herself how she could have been so stupid as not to have returned it to him the moment he gave it to her.

Similarly she should have known when he put his fingers under her chin what he was about to do.

It had however never entered her mind that a man she did not know and who had seen her for the first time would wish to kiss her.

Yet it was just the way, she told herself, that she would expect the Bucks and Beaux whom Peter was always talking about, to behave in London.

She should therefore have been on her guard from the moment she heard the man swearing in the lane, and should have guessed what he would be like when she saw his horse.

"I hate him!" she said aloud.

Then she found herself thinking that her first kiss was not in the least what she had expected.

She had always thought a kiss between two people would be something very soft and gentle.

Given with love and received with love, it would be something which reminded one of flowers, music and the first of the evening stars coming out in the sky.

Instead the stranger's lips had been hard and possessive and Hermia thought again that he had held her prisoner so that she would not escape.

"If that is a kiss," she exclaimed, "I want no more of them!"

Then she knew that was not true.

Of course she wanted to love and be loved.

It was all part of the stories she told herself in which the wildest adventures carried her to the top of the Himalayas or along crocodile-infested rivers in the centre of Africa.

Then the heroine would find the man of her dreams and they would be married.

Until now the hero had never had a face, but now she was certain of one thing: the man who had just kissed her was the villain in her stories.

As she thought about him and remembered his drooping eye-lids and the cynical twist to his lips, she was sure he not only looked like a villain but even more like the Devil.

'Perhaps that is who he was,' she thought as she picked up her basket of eggs and started to walk slowly homewards.

It was a fascinating thought, and she wondered what her mother would say if, when she arrived at the Vicarage, she told her she had met the Devil in Chanter's Lane, and he had kissed her.

Moreover if the Devil had done so, that meant she had now become a Witch.

She had so often heard whispered stories from the villagers of how in the dark woods which covered a great part of her uncle's estate Satanic revels took place to which foolish girls had been lured.

Nobody knew exactly what had happened to poor little Betsy. She had been sane before she went to one, but they said it was Satan himself who had sent her mad.

Her mother replied to such tales by saying that it was a lot of nonsense: Betsy had been born abnormal and her brain was damaged so that there was nothing the doctors could do for her.

But the villagers much preferred to believe that Betsy was Satan's child, and they enjoyed shivering apprehensively when she passed them.

If she was muttering, as she usually did, to herself, they were quite certain she was casting a curse on those she did not like.

There was also a story about another girl who had gone into the woods night after night, and finally had been spirited away so secretly that she was never seen again.

Hermia's father had given the explanation that as a visitor to the village who came from London had disappeared at exactly the same time, it was quite obvious what had happened.

But the villagers were convinced that the girl's fate was the same as Betsy's. She had joined in the Devil's revelries, and he had made her one of his own.

It seemed unlikely, Hermia thought, as she neared the village, that the Devil would ride such an outstanding, well-bred horse or would be dressed by the tailors patronised by the Prince Regent.

These were, Peter assured her, the only cutters who could make a man's coat fit as if he had been poured into it.

Thinking of Peter made Hermia wish that he was

at home. He would certainly think her experience amusing, but not even to her adored brother, to whom she confided almost everything, would she admit that she had been kissed by a stranger, Devil or no Devil.

"Peter would laugh at my being so foolish," she told herself, "while Papa would be furious!"

It was not often her good-natured, happy-go-lucky father was angry about anything.

But she had become aware this last year since she had grown up that he disliked the compliments that the Gentlemen who came to the Vicarage, although there were not many, paid her.

She had heard him say to her mother that it was a great impertinence and he was not going to tolerate it.

Although she knew it was very reprehensible Hermia had waited outside the door to overhear her mother's reply.

"Hermia is growing up, darling," she had said, "and as she is very pretty, in fact lovely, you must expect men to notice her, although unfortunately there are not many eligible bachelors around here to do so."

"I will not have any man whoever he may be, messing about with her," the Honourable Stanton Brooke said sharply.

"Nobody is likely to do that," Mrs. Brooke replied soothingly, "but I wish your brother and his wife would be a little kinder in asking her to some of the parties they give at the Hall. After all, she is the same age as Marilyn."

Hermia listening outside the door had given a little sigh and did not wait to hear any more.

She was well aware that her mother resented the fact that the Earl of Millbrooke, her father's brother, and his wife had almost ignored her since she was eighteen.

Not once had she been asked to any of the parties they gave at the Hall for her first cousin.

Hermia knew even better than her mother the reason for it.

Marilyn was jealous.

During the last year when they had done lessons together, as they had ever since they had been small children, she had grown more and more resentful of her cousin's looks and never missed an opportunity to disparage her.

Because she could not find anything unkind to say about her face she concentrated on her clothes.

"That gown you are wearing is almost in rags!" she would say when Hermia arrived at the Hall early in the morning. "I cannot think why you are content to make a scarecrow of yourself!"

"The answer is quite simple," Hermia would reply. "Your father is very rich and mine is very poor!"

She had not spoken resentfully, she had merely said it laughingly, but Marilyn had scowled and tried to think of another weapon with which she could hurt her.

It did seem to Hermia very unfair, even though her mother had explained to her, that it was traditional that the oldest son of the family should have everything, and the younger sons practically nothing.

"But why, Mama?"

"I will explain it to you," her mother had replied quietly. "Large estates like your Uncle John's must be passed intact from father to son. If they once started to divide up the land and the money amongst other members of the family there would soon be no great

Landlords in England, but only a lot of small holdings."

She paused to see if her daughter was listening to what she was saying before she went on:

"That is why in all the great aristocratic families the oldest son inherits everything, including the title. The second son generally goes into the Army or the Navy, while the third son becomes a Clergyman because there are always livings of which his father is the Patron."

"So that is why Papa became a Parson!"

Her mother had smiled.

"Exactly! I think in fact, if he had had the choice, he would rather have been a soldier. However, as you know, he is just a poor Parson, but a very, very good one."

That was true, Hermia knew, because her father for all his easy-going nature was extremely compassionate and had a real love of his fellow men.

He wanted to help everybody who came to him with their problems, and enjoyed doing so.

He would listen for hours, which she knew was something her uncle would never do, to the complaints of some poor old woman about her health, or to a farmer who was having difficulties with his crops.

If a young man found himself in trouble and did not know how to get out of it, her father would advise and help him, often financially.

"I never realised until I took Holy Orders," he had said once, "how many dramas take place in even the smallest village. If I were a writer, I could fill a book with the stories to which I listen every day, and sometimes that is what I think I will do."

"A very good idea, darling," his wife answered, "but as you spend all your free time at the moment riding, I think you will have to wait until you are too old to get on a horse before you start using your pen!"

The great joy of her father, apart from being at home with his wife and family, was to ride his brother's horses and hunt them in the winter.

The Earl was far more generous than his wife and it was the Countess who made it difficult, after Hermia had ceased to have lessons with Marilyn, for her to borrow the horses which filled the ample stables at the Hall and were usually under-exercised.

Her aunt was a plain woman and that partly accounted for her policy of more or less ostracising her husband's niece, besides her desire to protect her daughter from what she privately thought of as undesirable competition.

As it happened, Marilyn was quite pretty in a conventional way.

In fact, wearing gowns made by the most expensive dress-makers in Bond Street, and having her hair arranged by a very competent lady's-maid, she would have stood out in any Ball-Room if her cousin had not been present.

It was therefore, as the Countess of Millbrooke saw only too clearly, unlikely that Marilyn would receive the compliments that were her due if Hermia was present.

The first time Hermia realised she was not to be asked to a Ball that was to be given at the Hall and to which she had looked forward excitedly, she wept bitterly.

"How can Marilyn leave me out, Mama?" she had

sobbed. "We used to talk about what would happen when we were grown up and how we would share a Ball together."

She had given a little sob as she said:

"It all sounded such...f—fun, and we told each other how we would...count our...conquests and s—see who was the w—winner."

Her mother had put her arms around her and held her close.

"Now listen, my darling," she said. "You have to face the truth as I had to do when I married your father."

Hermia checked her tears and listened as her mother went on:

"You may have wondered sometimes," she began, "why your Aunt Edith, and sometimes even your Uncle John, are so condescending toward me."

"I had noticed that they give themselves airs and graces, Mama."

"That is because your grandfather had planned that your father should marry a very rich young woman," her mother explained, "who lived near the Hall in those days, and who had made it very clear that she loved your father."

Hermia smiled.

"That is not surprising, Mama! He is so good-looking that I can understand any woman thinking him fascinating."

"That is what I found," her mother said. "To me he is the most attractive, charming man in the whole world."

She spoke very softly and her eyes were tender as she went on:

"But I was the daughter of a General who had spent

his life serving his country, and retired with only a small pension which left him very little money for his children."

Hermia sat up and wiped the tears from her cheeks.

"Now I understand, Mama," she said. "Papa married you because he loved you and he was not interested in the girl with lots of money."

"That is exactly what happened," her mother said. "Your grandmother and your uncle pleaded with him to be sensible and think of the future, but he told them that was exactly what he was doing!"

"So you were married and lived happily ever afterward," Hermia said, her eyes shining.

"Very, very happily," her mother replied. "At the same time, darling, you have had to suffer for it, not only because you are my daughter, but also because you are very lovely."

Hermia was startled. It was something her mother had never said to her before.

"I am telling you the truth and not paying you a compliment," her mother said. "I believe it was because your father and I were so happy and so very much in love that both our children not only have beautiful faces, but beautiful characters as well."

That was certainly true of Peter, Hermia thought.

He was outstandingly handsome and because she resembled her mother she was aware that she was very pretty.

When there had been any sort of parties at the Hall all the male guests whatever their ages had always seemed to want to talk to her.

"You know," her mother had gone on reflectively, "we always have to pay for everything in life. Nothing is free, and you, darling, while you may find it a great advantage to be beautiful, will have to pay for it by knowing that other women will be jealous of you and will often make things difficult in consequence."

That was exactly what Marilyn had done, Hermia thought, when the invitations no longer came from the Hall, and her aunt looked at her with an expression of hostility even when they were in Church.

Peter had come down from Oxford—they had made great sacrifices to send him there—and talked not only of the exciting things he did as a student, but also of the visits he made to London with some of his friends.

When he was alone with Hermia he told her how much he resented not being able to afford the clothes his friends had from the best tailors.

"The horses they own," he went on, "are so outstanding that I will never be able to own anything to equal them!"

He, like his father, was allowed to ride the horses in the Earl's stables, but he could not take one away with him, and all he had at Oxford was what he could borrow from his friends, or hire from some livery stable.

"How I hate being poor!" he said angrily the last time he had been at home.

"Do not say that to Papa and Mama," Hermia warned quickly. "It would hurt them."

"I know it would," Peter replied, "but when I go up to the Hall and find William, with all the money in the world, sniping at me not only behind my back but to my face, and making disparaging remarks about me to my friends, I want to even things up by giving him a good hiding!"

Hermia gave a cry of horror.

"You must not do that! It would infuriate Uncle John and he might no longer allow you and Papa to ride his horses in future, and you know that I have been banned from the Hall."

"Papa told me," Peter replied, "but it is your own fault for being so ridiculously pretty!"

Hermia laughed.

"Are you paying me a compliment?"

"Of course I am!" Peter replied. "If you were dressed decently and allowed to go to London for a Season, you would be the toast of St. James's and I would be very proud of you!"

He was not only thinking of her, Hermia knew, but knowing that his richer friends, and especially his Cousin William, condescended to him and made it quite clear that he was "the poor man at their gates!"

Then because Peter was very like their father he said suddenly:

"To Hell with it! Why should I care? I intend to get the best out of life, and mark my words, Hermia, by hook or by crook, sooner or later I will have everything I want!"

"I believe you," Hermia replied, "if no one else does!"

Laughing they went down the stairs together hand-in-hand to eat the well-cooked but plain supper which was all their mother could afford from her house-keeping allowance which was a very modest one.

Now as Hermia walked in through the front door of the Vicarage she heard the clatter of pots and pans coming from the kitchen.

This meant that Nanny, who had looked after her

when she was a child and now did the cooking, would be annoyed because she had taken so long in fetching the eggs.

She wondered if she should tell her the real reason, then as she walked in through the kitchen door Nanny said:

"It's about time! I suppose you've been day-dreaming as usual, and here am I trying to have a meal ready for your father before he sets out to see that Mrs. Grainger, who's sent for him!"

"I am sorry if I have been a long time, Nanny," Hermia said.

"Your head's always in the clouds!" Nanny snapped. "One of these days you'll forget your way home, that's what you'll do!"

She took the basket from Hermia, put it on the table, and started to break several of the eggs into a bowl preparatory to making an omelette.

"Why does Mrs. Grainger want to see Papa?" Hermia asked curiously.

"I expect she thinks she's dying again!" Nanny replied tartly. "Any excuse to have the Vicar holding her hand and telling her God's waiting for her with all His angels. I should have thought myself He had something better to do!"

Hermia laughed.

Nanny's caustic remarks were always different from what anybody else would say, but she knew it was because the old woman loved them all and resented their father, as she considered it, being 'put upon.'

"Now, go and lay the table, please, Miss Hermia," she said. "I'm not letting your father out of this house with an empty stomach, whatever he may say!"

Hermia ran to obey orders, and she had just laid

the table in the Dining-Room for the three of them when she heard her mother come back from the village.

It always seemed extraordinary in such a small place that there was so much to do and so many people who wanted either her mother or her father to help them.

It resulted in there hardly being an hour in the day when they were all at home together.

Now as Mrs. Brooke came in through the front door and saw her daughter in the Dining-Room she exclaimed:

"Oh, darling, I am glad you are here! I have had such a difficult time with poor Mrs. Burles, and I promised I would send her some of my special cough mixture. I wonder if, after luncheon, you would take it to her?"

"Of course, Mama," Hermia agreed.

Her mother paused at the open door and said:

"Did you fetch the eggs from Honeysuckle Farm? And has Mrs. Johnson any news of her son?"

"No, she has not heard from him," Hermia replied.

Her mother looked sad, and for the first time Hermia wondered how many people would take so much interest in the trouble and difficulties of those around them as her father and mother did.

If somebody's child was ill, an old person died, or there was no news of a boy in one of the Services, it became to them a personal problem.

In fact, Hermia often thought that the villagers' joy was their joy, their grief their grief.

It was like being part of an enormous family, she told herself, and knew that life was very different for other people who like her Aunt and Uncle were surrounded by a number of acquaintances, none of whom were really of any consequence to them.

Then she could not help feeling a little ache in her heart because Marilyn was no longer her friend, but only a relation who had no wish to see her any more.

It had been very different when they were children and competed with one another at their lessons.

They had found innumerable things to do, both within the huge rambling old house which had been in the Brooke family for generations, and outside in the well-kept gardens, but most of all in the stables.

The Earl had not married until he was older than was usual, with the result that his younger brother had a daughter almost the same age as his own, so that it was natural that the first cousins should be more or less brought up together.

This had been a great advantage to Hermia's mother and father.

At the same time, she thought, it had made her acutely conscious of the difference there was between her Uncle's position and their own.

She was not very old however, before she realised that the most important difference lay in the happiness which seemed to make the small Vicarage always full of sunshine, while at the Hall she was aware that there was an atmosphere which was gloomy and often oppressive.

A few years later she understood that her Uncle and Aunt did not get on together.

In public they put a very good face on it, and when entertaining guests always referred to each other politely, and in a manner that only somebody perceptive would have been aware was insincere.

But when there was nobody there except for Marilyn and herself, it was quite obvious that the Countess found her husband extremely exasperating, while he, who was on the whole an easy-going man, disliked almost everything his wife suggested.

This meant there was a tension between them that was very obvious to anybody as sensitive and perceptive as Hermia.

When there were no guests in the house the two girls had luncheon downstairs.

But often Hermia would much rather have been at home eating the simple food that Nanny prepared rather than the rich, exotic dishes that were served by a Butler and three footmen at the Hall.

Then when she reached home in the evening, Hermia would fling her arms round her mother's neck and say with the spontaneity of a child:

"I love you, Mama, I love being with you, and I love this small, warm house when we are all here together."

Because Mrs. Brooke understood what her daughter was feeling, she went out of her way to explain how important it was that Hermia should study and learn everything she could from the experienced and expensive Governesses whom her Uncle engaged.

"I am afraid, darling," she said, "if you did not go to the Hall for lessons, you would have to be taught some subjects by Papa, which would be very spasmodic because he would either forget or be too busy!"

Hermia laughed knowing that this was true.

"Or," her mother continued, "we should have to persuade poor old Miss Cunningham, who was a Governess once, but is now almost blind, to help you with the other things you must learn."

"I understand what you are saying to me, Mama,"

Hermia had replied, when she was fourteen, "and I am very grateful for everything Miss Wade can teach me. At the same time, I know it is more important even than my lessons that I am allowed to use the Library at the Hall."

She gave a little laugh before she added:

"Uncle John's Curator said that nobody else is interested in the books except me, and when he makes a list of what is required for the Library I am sure he includes books which he knows I will enjoy."

"Then you are very, very lucky," Mrs. Brooke smiled.

That was another privilege which Hermia was done out of.

It would not have been difficult for her to go to the Library, especially when her uncle and aunt were away.

But she felt it was wrong to make use of their books if they did not want her personally.

She told herself proudly that somehow she would manage, as Peter was going to do, to get what she wanted without relying on her relatives.

When luncheon was finished her father hurried off to keep his appointment, driving an old-fashioned gig, having between the shafts a spirited young horse he had recently bought cheaply from one of the farmers.

Hermia picked up the bottle of cough mixture her mother had made and started to walk to the cottage where Mrs. Burles lived.

Her mother's healing herbs which she made into salves and lotions were famous in the village.

But Hermia suspected that the old gossips who talked about the Devil's revelries in the woods were sure the Vicar's wife was a White Witch.

"Yer mother's a miracle worker!" one of the villagers had said to Hermia last week, "or else hers got some special magic of her own!"

She had looked at Hermia with an expression in her eyes as she spoke which told her exactly what she was thinking.

"Mama believes that God gave us in nature the cure for every ill," she said firmly. "Just as a nettle stings us, so He made the dockleaf to take away the pain."

It was an argument she had used before, but she knew the woman to whom she was speaking did not want to hear it.

"Magic, that's what yer mother has," she said firmly, "and when I puts the salve her sent me on th' burn I had on me hand, an' very ugly it were, it disappeared overnight!"

Hermia smiled.

"I think you can thank the bees for that," she said, "because there was honey in the salve."

She knew even as she spoke what the woman was thinking, and nothing she could say would dispel the idea that it was super-natural magic which had cured her burn.

It was not surprising, Hermia told herself, that the people living in the small thatched cottages with their tiny gardens had nothing better to talk about.

The village green with the pond in the centre of it, the black and white Inn with its ancient clients drinking ale in pewter mugs, were the only centres of activity except for the small grey stone Church.

Nothing ever happened in Little Brookfield, which of course had been named after the Brooke family who lived at the 'Big House.'

The Earl owned the land, the farm, the cottages, employed the young and healthy and of course, paid the stipend of the Vicar who ministered to their spiritual needs.

"They want to believe in super-natural things," Hermia told herself.

If she was honest, she herself believed in the fairies, goblins, nymphs, and elves which had all been part of the stories her mother had told her when she was a child.

She still thought about them, because they seemed so real and so much part of the countryside.

When she was in the great woods it was easy to think there were elves and goblins burrowing under the trees.

She was sure there were nymphs like the morning mist rising from the dark pond in the centre of one wood where she would often go when she wanted to be alone and think.

In the spring there would be a vision of bluebells that were so lovely that she would feel they were enchanted, and after the bluebells would come primroses and violets.

Then the birds would begin to build their nests in the trees overhead and the rabbits would move about in the undergrowth.

Red squirrels would scurry away at her approach, then stop to stare at her curiously, as if they wondered how she dared to intrude on what was their secret domain.

It was all so beautiful that she had no wish to believe in anything ugly or frightening.

Then she thought of the man who had kissed her

this morning, and wondered if perhaps he had ridden into the heart of the wood on his fine horse, and disappeared because he was not a human being.

To think of him made her anger well up inside her as she remembered that in the pocket of her gown there was still the golden guinea he had given her.

She had forgotten about it when she had been laying the table for the luncheon and when they had laughed and talked while they had eaten.

Now after she had given old Mrs. Burles her 'magic cough lotion' she walked back towards the Church.

It was very near the Vicarage, in fact just on the other side of the road, and she slipped in through the porch that needed repairing and walked onto the ancient flagged floor.

The Church was very old, having stood there for nearly three hundred years.

Every time Hermia attended a Service she could feel the vibrations and prayers of those who had worshipped here and had left a part of themselves behind.

Her father believed the same.

"Thoughts are never wasted and never erased," he had said once.

"What do you mean by that, Papa?"

"When we think of something, and of course when we pray," the Vicar replied, "we send it out as if it had wings on the air. It is carried up by our vibrations, or perhaps by something stronger that we do not understand, into eternity."

"I think that is a terrifying idea!" Hermia protested. "I shall be very careful what I think in the future!"

Her father had laughed.

"You cannot stop thinking any more than you can

stop breathing," he said, "and I am honestly convinced that wherever we have been, we leave our thoughts and the life force we give them."

Hermia had understood that he was thinking as he spoke of the atmosphere in the Church which she had always known was so vivid, so strong that she never felt as if she was alone there.

There were always other people with her, people whom she could not see, but who had lived in Little Brookfield.

They had taken their sorrows and their happiness into the Church, and their feelings had been bequeathed to the small building for ever.

They had given the Church, she thought, exactly the sanctity that people expected in a House of God, and she could feel it now as she walked in through the door.

It was there to welcome her and to make her feel that she was not alone, but enveloped by a love that could protect, help and inspire her whenever she had need of it.

As she drew the guinea from her pocket she felt as if there were unseen people around her who understood why she was putting it in the poor-box.

She knew what a lot of good her father would do with it.

She slipped it through the slit in the box and heard the sharp sound it made as it fell to the bottom.

Then as she knelt in one of the ancient oak pews to pray, she looked up at the altar.

The flowers which her mother had arranged the previous Saturday were still a brilliant patch of colour, and Hermia felt a strange joy sweep over her.

"Make something happen for me, God," she prayed.

"I want to have a fuller life than what I am living at the moment."

As she prayed she almost felt as if she grew wings which would carry her away as her thoughts did, and she could visualise herself flying out into the great world outside of which she knew so little.

There would be mountains to climb like those in her stories, rivers to negotiate, and seas to sail over.

"Give me all that, please, God!" she finished.

Then as she rose to her feet she thought it was too demanding a request and God, like her father, would tell her to be content with her lot as it was.

"I am so lucky that I have . . . so much," she tried to tell herself philosophically.

But she knew it was not enough.

chapter two

WHEN Hermia arrived back at the Vicarage it was to find the house empty.

She knew that Nanny had gone shopping, and her father and mother were both visiting people who had asked for their help.

It was actually quite surprising that she had not been left a mass of instructions concerning other things to do.

With a feeling of delight she thought that this was an opportunity to continue reading a book that she was finding absorbingly interesting.

Usually the only time she had to read was when she went to bed at night, but as she was often too tired to do anything but sleep she had so far only read one chapter.

Now she brought her book down from her Bedroom and curling herself up in the window-seat in the

Sitting-Room she found her place and started to read.

She was concentrating so intently on the book on her knees that she started when the door of the Sitting-Room opened.

She turned her head impatiently thinking it was Nanny who would undoubtedly want her to fetch something like mint from the garden, or perhaps cut a lettuce for supper.

Then she saw to her astonishment her Cousin Marilyn come into the room.

She was looking exceedingly smart in a gown which Hermia knew was in the very latest fashion.

Gowns during the war had been very plain and straight, and most people, however rich they might be, wore white muslins.

This material in fact sometimes verged on the indecent because it was inclined to cling to the figure, revealing not only the wearer's curves, but sometimes how little was being worn underneath.

Now far more luxurious materials were available and the bodice and sleeves of the gowns were either embroidered or trimmed with lace.

Marilyn's gown had three rows of lace round the hem.

Her bonnet had the high tilted brim which Hermia had seen illustrated in *The Ladies' Journal,* and the satin ribbons under her chin and round her high waist could only have come from Paris.

For a moment she could only stare at her cousin thinking it strange that she should call at the Vicarage herself rather than send a message, which was almost a command, for her to come to the Hall.

Then she scrambled to her feet saying:

"Marilyn! What a surprise! I have not seen you for such a long time!"

Marilyn did not look in the least embarrassed, although she was well aware she had not bothered to speak to Hermia since Christmas, and she merely replied:

"I have been very busy, but now I want your help."

"My help?" Hermia repeated in astonishment.

Of all the people who came to the Vicarage for help she would have thought the last person to ask the assistance of either her or her father or mother, would have been Marilyn.

The Countess had always made it very clear that she thought that what she called 'slaving after the lower classes' was a waste of time.

"You do not suppose they are grateful to you," Hermia had heard her say once to her father. "From all I hear of such people they take everything for granted and complain that one does not do more for them."

"That is not true of my flock," Hermia heard her father object. "In fact, when Elizabeth was ill last year, we were both tremendously touched by the little presents brought her every day, and the way they prayed for her recovery."

The Countess had merely sniffed, but Hermia knew her mother had been deeply moved at the way the whole village had worried over her.

They had so little themselves, but they wanted to share what they could with her.

Sometimes it was only a fresh brown egg they thought she would like for her breakfast, a bunch of flowers from their gardens, or from those who were more practical, a comb of golden honey.

Hermia had known, though her father could never have made the Countess understand, that it was not the material things which mattered so much as the understanding and sympathy which came from the heart.

Now as she walked towards her cousin Hermia thought a little apprehensively that while Marilyn was looking very attractive in her elegant clothes, there was a contemptuous expression in her eyes.

She did not attempt to kiss Hermia, but merely looked around the room, selected the most comfortable chair, and sat down in it a little gingerly as if she felt its legs might be unsound and would collapse under her.

Hermia sat down on a stool that stood in front of the fireplace, moving as she did so some sewing her mother had been doing before she went out.

She knew that Marilyn thought it was untidy of her to have left it there.

Almost as if she was looking through her cousin's eyes Hermia was suddenly aware that the carpet was threadbare, the curtains were faded, and one of the brass handles which had come off the soft table in a corner of the room had not been replaced.

Then she lifted her chin proudly and told herself that whatever Marilyn might be thinking she would not exchange the shabby Vicarage which was filled with love and happiness for all the luxury of the Hall.

Then she looked at her cousin wondering what she had to say.

"I suppose I can trust you," Marilyn said, and her voice had a harsh note in it that Hermia did not miss.

"Trust me?" she questioned. "I do not know what you mean."

"I have to trust somebody to do what I want," Marilyn replied, "and I cannot believe that being a Parson's daughter you would do anything underhand or what Papa would call 'unsportsmanlike.'"

Hermia stiffened.

Then as she was about to defend herself she bit back the words to say quietly:

"We have known each other for eighteen years, Marilyn. If you do not know what I am like by this time, then there is nothing I can say to convince you I am anything but what I am!"

As if she did not wish to annoy her Marilyn said quickly:

"No, no, of course not! I am only a little apprehensive about what I want to ask you to do."

Hermia thought she could understand that.

She had not seen her cousin since five months ago, and then it had only been for the family Christmas dinner.

If there was one thing the household at the Vicarage all disliked it was the Christmas dinner which took place every year at the Hall.

Although it was the season of good will, Christmas Day celebrating the birth of Christ, was always a very busy one for the Vicar, involving a great number of Services in his Church.

He also visited several people in their homes if they were too ill or infirm to come to Church.

"I am dead tired," Hermia had heard her father say last Christmas when it was time to go out for dinner. "What I would like to do, my darling, is to sit with you and the children in front of the fire and drink a glass of port."

Her mother had laughed.

"There will be plenty to drink at the Hall."

"And plenty of snide remarks to listen to," her father replied.

Because of the way he spoke her mother had risen to sit on the arm of his chair and smooth his hair back from his square forehead.

"I know it is a bore, darling, that we have to go there, and Edith is certain to make things difficult for both of us, but I think in his heart your brother looks forward to seeing you."

"John is all right," the Vicar replied, "but I find his wife intolerable, his son a stuck-up young cock's-comb, and although Marilyn was a sweet little girl of whom I was very fond, she has grown into a very conceited young woman!"

Because of the critical way he spoke which was so unlike him, his wife had laughed as if she could not help it.

Then she said:

"'What cannot be cured must be endured,' as Nanny would say, and we will not stay long. But do not forget that you are hunting tomorrow and as it is on one of your brother's horses, you have to pay for the privilege."

"I love you!" the Vicar replied. "You always put things in the right perspective, and I will put up with a lot of disagreeableness from Edith so long as Peter and I can be mounted on those excellent horses of his."

As she went up to change for dinner Hermia had thought her mother had been right in saying one never got anything for nothing in the world.

Like her father she had found the Christmas dinner since she had grown up a very uncomfortable evening.

She knew that her aunt, and Marilyn for that matter, would look her up and down in her cheap evening-gown which was the best her father could afford.

They would contrive to make her feel as if she was the Goose-Girl who had got into the King's Palace by mistake.

Then as if Marilyn wished to impress upon her how important she was now that she had been to London, she had reeled off her successes one by one.

Like a child showing another how much bigger her toys were, she was determined Hermia should be suitably impressed.

Because she had never heard of the grand people of whom Marilyn spoke, it was not a particularly edifying conversation, and while she appeared to listen her attention was wandering to where she knew Peter was suffering in the same way from his Cousin William.

The Viscount, dressed as a very 'Tulip of Fashion,' would be endeavouring, as Peter had expressed it savagely on the way home, to turn him into a country yokel.

"The only consolation," he said to Hermia, "is that while I am absolutely certain I shall get my Degree at Oxford, William is so busy drinking at all the Clubs that he will undoubtedly fail. What is more, he was very nearly sent down last term."

Hermia slipped her hand into her brother's.

"You must not worry about what he says to you," she answered. "He is jealous because you look better and you ride better than he does, and if I were one of the Beauties he tells us he pursues in London, I should find him a dead bore!"

Peter threw back his head and laughed, but Hermia

knew she had spoken nothing but the truth.

Compared with Peter, William was a plain young man with eyes too close together and a long upper lip which he had inherited from his mother's family.

He was not a particularly good horseman, and he found it distinctly annoying that when they were hunting his Cousin Peter was always in the front of the field and sailed over the highest hedges with ease.

William was often left behind despite the fact that he had the pick of his father's best horses.

Last Christmas Hermia remembered had been the least enjoyable of any dinner they had ever had at the Hall.

Because Marilyn had been particularly unpleasant towards her that evening, it was all the more surprising that she should be here at this moment asking for her help.

She sat on the stool waiting and had the idea that her cousin was finding it rather difficult to put what she wanted of her into words.

Then as if she felt that first she must make herself more pleasant than usual, she remarked:

"I can see, Hermia, that you have grown out of that gown you are wearing! It is too tight and too short! I suppose I might have thought of it before, but I have quite a number of gowns that I can no longer wear which I might as well pass on to you."

For a moment Hermia stiffened.

It flashed through her mind that she would rather wear rags and tatters than be an object of Marilyn's charity.

Then she told herself that was a very selfish attitude.

It was a struggle for her father and mother to afford

the material for one new gown between them when any money that could be spared for clothes was spent on Peter.

Only last night Peter had said to her mother when her father was out of the room:

"Do you think there is any chance, Mama, of my having a new riding-coat? I am ashamed of the one I am wearing now, and since I have the chance to compete in the Steeple-Chase that is taking place at Blenheim Palace, I have no wish for you to be ashamed of me."

Her mother had smiled.

"You know I would never be that, and I noticed the other day how worn your coat was. I am sure Papa and I can manage to find enough money for a new one."

Peter put his arms round his mother and kissed her.

"You are a brick!" he said. "I know how little you and Papa spend on yourselves, and I feel rather like the Importunate Widow."

Her mother had laughed.

"You will have your riding-coat, dearest. We will find the money for it one way or another!"

Hermia had known that this meant the gown her mother had been planning for herself would not materialise, nor would the new bonnet she had been promised as soon as they could afford it.

It all flashed through her mind and she said quickly:

"It would be very, very kind of you, Marilyn, if you would send me anything you have no further use of. You know quite well it is always a struggle for Papa and Mama, even though they are as economical as possible."

"I will tell my lady's-maid to pack up everything

I no longer want," Marilyn promised. "Now, Hermia, let me tell you what I want from you."

"What is it?"

"I must explain first that we have a very important guest staying with us."

Hermia's eyes were on her cousin's face as she went on:

"It is the Marquis of Deverille, and to express myself frankly—I intend to marry him!"

Hermia gave a little cry.

"Oh, Marilyn, how exciting! Are you very much in love with him?"

"It is not a question of whether I love him or not," Marilyn replied. "The Marquis of Deverille is without exception the most important matrimonial catch in the whole of London!"

"Why is he so important?" Hermia asked curiously.

"Because he is rich, and because of his position. He has houses and estates which, like his race-horses, are better than anybody else's."

"I think I have heard Papa speak of him," Hermia said wrinkling her brow.

"It is very unlikely that Uncle Stanton would know the Marquis," Marilyn said quickly. "He moves only in the most exalted circles, and his race-horses win all the Classic Races, so that he is acclaimed wherever he goes."

She gave a little sigh and said in a voice that sounded very human:

"As his wife I would have a position that would be almost Royal! Everybody would be extremely envious that I had managed to capture him."

"And do you think he would make you happy?" Hermia asked.

Marilyn hesitated before she replied:

"I would be very, very happy to be the Marchioness of Deverille, and that is what I am determined to be!"

There was a hard note in her voice which Hermia knew only too well.

When Marilyn made up her mind about anything it was always more comfortable for everybody concerned to let her have it immediately.

When she was a child she had found her tantrums would upset her Nurse and Governess to the point where they decided it was pointless not to give way to her.

Hermia knew only too well that behind a very pretty face there was a steel-like will.

This had meant, when they were in the School-Room together, that if Marilyn found the lessons boring she just refused to listen to anything the Governess said.

She would flounce out of the room leaving Hermia alone with a flustered teacher who had no idea how she could control such an obstreperous pupil.

Because Hermia had been anxious to learn everything she could even when she was quite young, she smoothed down the elderly woman who had been insulted and coaxed her into continuing the lesson so that she could learn what she wanted to know.

She thought now that if Marilyn had made up her mind to marry the Marquis, or any other man, he would have great difficulty in escaping from her.

Then she thought that was rather an unkind thing to think and she said softly:

"If you marry the man you love, Marilyn, I can only wish you all the happiness in the world!"

"I thought you would say that," Marilyn replied,

"and that means you will have to help me to win him."

"He has not proposed to you?"

"No, of course not! The minute he proposes to me I shall put it into the *Gazette* before he can change his mind, and every unmarried woman in London will be wanting to scratch my eyes out for succeeding where they have failed!"

"Is he very attractive, and do you love him very much?" Hermia asked softly.

"At this moment I find him extremely elusive and somewhat unresponsive," Marilyn said, almost as if she were speaking to herself. "He accepted Papa's invitation to stay, and while I know it was more to see the new mares that Papa has imported from the Continent than to be with me, I have made the very most of having him at the Hall."

Now Marilyn was speaking in the way she used to before they grew up, and as if once again she was thinking of her cousin as somebody very close to her, she said:

"I have to win him, Hermia! You do see I have to make him propose to me! But it is not going to be easy!"

"Why not?" Hermia asked. "You look very, very pretty, Marilyn, and I cannot believe that he would stay at the Hall and not be interested in you."

"That is what I would like to think," Marilyn confided. "At the same time, he is fawned on by all the most beautiful women in London."

She paused, then said as if she was speaking to herself:

"Of course they are all married, but the Marquis will have to marry some day in order to produce an heir. I have heard rumors that he bitterly dislikes his cousin who will inherit if he has no son."

"I am sure he will want to marry you," Hermia said reassuringly.

There was silence as if Marilyn was thinking it over before she said:

"I was told in confidence by one of his relatives that they have all been begging the Marquis on their knees for the last five years to marry and have a family."

"Does it matter if he does not?" Hermia asked.

"Do not be silly, Hermia! I have just told you that he hates the cousin who would succeed him, and so do his sisters, his aunts, his grandmother and everybody else in the Deverille family."

"What is wrong with his cousin that they hate him so much?" Hermia enquired curiously.

"I have never met him," Marilyn replied, "but they say he is always disgustingly drunk and spends his time hanging round very disreputable actresses."

She gave a little laugh.

"Nobody would ever expect the Marquis to behave like that, for he is very conscious of his own consequence! But he has been disillusioned through having a very unfortunate affair when he was a young man."

"What happened?" Hermia asked.

She felt this was almost like one of the stories she told herself and everything that Marilyn was telling her she found intensely interesting.

Marilyn shrugged her shoulders.

"I do not know all the details, but I gather it happened when he was very young, and it has given him a very poor opinion of women, and in consequence he is far more interested in his horses!"

She drew in her breath before she went on:

"But he has to marry, and I am determined that I shall be his wife!"

"And I am sure you will be, dearest," Hermia said, "but I do not see how I can help you."

"That is what I am going to tell you."

Marilyn's voice grew more intense as she said:

"The Marquis was talking to Papa at dinner last night and he was saying that he thought things had changed a great deal since the war. Noble families because they were hard-up or could not attend to their estates as they used to, were not looking after their people as his father had done when he was alive."

Marilyn glanced at her cousin to see that Hermia's blue eyes were fixed on her face with rapt attention and she continued:

"'My father,' the Marquis said, 'knew the name of every man he employed, just as he knew the names of his fox-hounds, and my mother called at every cottage on our estate. If somebody was ill she took them soup and medicine, and when the children grew up she found them employment, either on our own land or with one of our relatives.'"

It flashed through Hermia's mind that was what her father and mother did in a very small way.

Marilyn continued:

"'Nobody appears to behave like that today,' the Marquis said, 'and I therefore understand why the labourers are dissatisfied in the North and there is a great deal of dissention, I am told, in the Southern Counties.'"

Marilyn paused and asked:

"Now do you understand what I want?"

She saw Hermia was looking bewildered, and the sharpness was back in her voice as she said:

"Do not be silly, Hermia! I have to convince him that, like his mother, I am interested in the people on the estate and help them."

"But, Marilyn . . ." Hermia began, then stopped.

She had been about to say that in all the years she had known her cousin she had never known her take the slightest interest in anybody on the estate.

What was more, the Countess had always sneered at the way her father and mother spent so much time looking after the people in the village.

Once when the Earl had had a man dismissed because his agent had reported his work was shoddy and he was taking a long time over it, her father had pleaded with his brother to give the man a second chance.

"He is sick," he explained, "and cannot afford to stay at home and lose his wages. His wife is expecting another baby and there are three small children in the house."

The Earl had refused to listen.

"I leave all those things to my Farm Manager," he said. "I never interfere!"

It was her father, Hermia remembered, who had kept the man and his family alive out of his own pocket and had by some miracle found him another job with a wage that had at least saved them from starvation.

Hermia knew this was just one example of what often happened on the estate and that her father, although he never said so, deplored his brother's indifference and lack of interest in the people he employed.

"I cannot think what you want me to do for you, Marilyn," she said apprehensively.

42

"I have thought it all out," Marilyn said, "and all you have to do is exactly what I tell you."

"I will do it if it is possible," Hermia said.

"It is quite possible," Marilyn replied. "Now listen..."

She bent forward and lowered her voice almost as if she was afraid of being overheard.

"I have decided that I will accompany the Marquis tomorrow morning when he goes riding. I know neither Papa nor William intend to ride early, but the Marquis likes to ride before breakfast."

Hermia raised her eye-brows.

"I have never known you to be up before breakfast!" she said.

"I am quite prepared to get up at dawn if I have good reason to!" Marilyn declared. "Now listen to what I am saying..."

"I am listening."

"I shall join him in the stables and suggest we ride towards Bluebell Wood. You know how pretty and romantic that is!"

"Yes... of course," Hermia agreed.

"I shall be there at about half after seven," Marilyn went on, "and we will ride slowly through the wood. Then I want you to come galloping in search of me."

"Me?" Hermia exclaimed.

"Just listen!" Marilyn snapped. "You will come riding as quickly as you can and say to me:

"'Oh, Marilyn, I have been looking for you! Poor old Mrs. "Thingumabob" is dying, but she says she cannot die until she can say goodbye to you and thank you for all your kindness to her!'"

Hermia stared at her cousin in disbelief.

43

It seemed a strange way for Marilyn to try to impress the Marquis and she did not think it would sound very plausible.

Almost as if her cousin read her thoughts Marilyn said:

"You can put it in your own words, but make it sound convincing and urgent as if the woman were really crying out for me."

"I . . . I will do my best," Hermia said, "but what happens . . . then?"

"I have thought it out carefully," Marilyn answered. "I shall exclaim: 'Oh, poor Mrs. "Thingumabob!" Of course I must go to her!' I shall start to ride away, but in case the Marquis should attempt to follow me I shall say to you:

"'Show His Lordship the way home!' Then before he can accompany me, as he will obviously wish to do, I shall be almost out of sight."

"Supposing he insists upon following you?" Hermia asked.

"Then you must somehow prevent him from doing so," Marilyn said. "I shall ride towards the village, then go slowly back to the house by a different way so that no one will see me."

Her lips curved in a little smile as she said:

"Later I will tell the Marquis how a poor old woman died happily because I was holding her hand, and he will realise that I am just like his mother, and that I care about the people on the estate."

Now there was silence, and after a moment Marilyn said:

"Well, what do you think of my idea? It cannot be very difficult for you to play the part I have asked of you!"

"N—no . . . of course . . . not," Hermia said. "I am just . . . hoping that the Marquis will . . . believe you."

"Why should he doubt it?" Marilyn asked aggressively. "And if he does, it will be entirely your fault!"

"Please . . . do not say that," Hermia pleaded. "You know I will try in every way I can to sound as if somebody really is on their . . . death-bed, just as they always send for Mama . . . but . . ."

Her voice died away.

She knew she could not express in words that she felt it unlikely that any man, unless he was very stupid, would believe that Marilyn really cared for anybody except herself.

Then she was ashamed of being so ungenerous!

She told herself she would try very, very hard to persuade the Marquis that the people on the estate looked to her cousin for comfort and consolation in their troubles.

She still had a feeling it was not going to be easy, but because it was something she knew she could not put into words she merely said simply:

"I will do what you ask, Marilyn, but you are aware I have no horse to ride at the moment, and it might seem strange if I fetched one from your stables."

"I will send you a groom with a horse late this evening, so that your father will not be aware of it," Marilyn replied.

"I shall enjoy riding it," Hermia said with a smile.

She glanced at her cousin and now saw an expression in her eyes she had seen before.

"There will be no reason for you to stay long with the Marquis," Marilyn said sharply. "You must give me just time enough to get out of sight, point the way back to the Hall, and then follow me."

"I will do that," Hermia agreed.

"And what is more, you need not doll yourself up because you are meeting the sort of Gentleman you are never likely to see in Little Brookfield!"

"No . . . of course not," Hermia answered.

"If there were anybody else I could trust, I would not ask you."

"That is an unkind thing to say!"

"I cannot help it," her cousin answered. "You are too pretty, Hermia, and it has made me hate you ever since I knew that however expensively I were dressed you would always look better than I do."

Hermia made a little gesture with her hands before she said:

"We also used to have such happy times when we were young, and I miss them, Marilyn . . . I miss them very much!"

"If that is an attempt to coax me into asking you to the parties we give now that I am grown up," Marilyn replied, "I am not having you there! I have seen the expression in Gentlemen's eyes when they look at you, and I am not so stupid as to want that sort of competition."

"I realise that," Hermia said, "and I cannot help my looks. But since you yourself are very, very pretty, Marilyn, I am quite certain you will capture your Marquis."

"That is what I intend to do."

Hermia was silent for a moment. Then she said:

"I do not believe love depends so much on people's looks. Mama said once that having a pretty face was only a good introduction! I think that when people begin to fall in love with each other, there must be many of other factors to attract them. rather than just the outward appearance of the person in whom they are interested."

"If you are preaching to me about having a kind heart, a compassionate nature, and a love for old people and animals," Marilyn retorted, "I am not going to listen!"

Hermia laughed because she sounded just like the petulant little girl she had been when they used to quarrel in the Nursery.

Marilyn went on:

"I am quite content with myself as I am. The only thing I am concerned with is getting married, and making sure that my husband is the most important man available."

"Papa always says that if you want something badly enough, with willpower and prayer you will get it."

Unexpectedly Marilyn laughed.

"I am sure Uncle Stanton would be delighted to know that I am in fact praying I will get the Marquis, and I shall be extremely angry if my prayers are not answered!"

"I am sure they will be," Hermia said soothingly. "And I can think of nobody, Marilyn, who would look lovelier wearing a coronet."

"That is what I intend to have," Marilyn said, "and the smartest wedding that has been seen in London for years!"

It flashed through Hermia's mind that the one person she would not ask to be a bride's-maid was herself.

Marilyn was however already rising to her feet, and pulling her elaborately decorated skirt into place.

"Now do not make any mistakes, Hermia, about what you have to do!" she admonished. "We should reach the Bluebell Wood at about twenty minutes to eight o'clock. I can make all sorts of excuses to linger in the centre of it, but you had better not keep me waiting too long!"

"I will be there, I promise you," Hermia said, "and do not forget the horse. It would not be so impressive if I arrived on foot, which is my only means of transport these days."

"I realise you are reproaching me in a very obvious manner for not allowing you to ride Papa's horses," Marilyn said. "The truth is, Hermia, you ride too well, and I am sick of hearing the grooms and everybody else say that I should ride like you."

There was nothing Hermia could say to this, and there was silence as her cousin walked towards the door.

"Be exactly on time," Marilyn said as she walked into the hall, "and I will repay you by remembering to send you the clothes I have promised you."

It was difficult for Hermia to refrain from saying proudly that she could keep them.

Instead she forced herself to answer gently and without the slightest note of sarcasm in her voice:

"It is very kind of you, Marilyn dear, and both Mama and I will be very, very grateful."

She walked to the front door with her cousin as she spoke, to see an elegant open carriage with a coachman and a footman on the box standing outside.

When they saw Hermia they both touched their cockaded hats and grinned at her.

She had known the coachman since she was a little girl, and the footman was a lad from the village.

He jumped down in order to open the door of the carriage for Marilyn and carefully placed a light rug over her knees.

As he clambered back up onto the box the horses started off and Marilyn raised her gloved hand with a graceful gesture of goodbye.

Hermia had a last glimpse of her pretty beribboned bonnet passing through the drive-gate which was sadly in need of a coat of paint.

Then she went back into the house thinking that Marilyn's visit was like one of her fairy-stories.

It was hard to believe it had happened or that she had been asked to take part in what seemed a ridiculous charade.

She could understand Marilyn's reasoning and her motive in working out what seemed a very complicated plot to capture the Marquis of Deverille, but privately she had her doubts as to whether she would be successful.

A great love, if that was what she was asking from the man who would want to marry her, should not be based on something that seemed on second thoughts rather theatrical and contrived.

Hermia had the uncomfortable suspicion that if the Marquis was at all intelligent and intuitive he would remember the conversation they had had at dinner about his mother.

Would he not therefore think it a strange coincidence that two days later Marilyn should be called to a dying woman's bedside?

Hermia felt sure that if she were in the Marquis's position she would certainly think it very strange.

But the Marquis might be different.

If he was a stupid man, beguiled by Marilyn's pretty face, the suggestion that she was like his mother might swing the scales in her favour.

She picked up her book again from where she had

discarded it when Marilyn arrived.

She did not open it. Instead she looked out of the window at the beauty of the unkept garden with the shrubs just coming into bloom.

The blossom on the fruit trees gave them a fairy-like appearance that swept her into one of the stories she had known as a child where the spirits of the trees danced at night under the stars.

Then she knew that if she ever fell in love, as she prayed she would one day, she would never stoop to scheming or intriguing to encourage the man on whom she had set her heart into proposing to her.

Either he would want her because he recognised her as the woman he loved, through time and space, or else whatever she might feel for him she would let him go.

Then she would hide her tears privately so that he would never be aware of how much she cared.

"It is humiliating and degrading to ensnare a man as if he were a wild animal," she told herself fiercely.

Then she found herself once again thinking of the man with a face like the Devil who had kissed her and pressed a guinea into her hand.

She told herself that the kisses she had dreamt of and imagined in her stories were very different from the one he had given her.

She was sure that if ever she received them they would not be disappointing.

chapter three

HERMIA rose very early and put on the riding-skirt she had made herself.

She remembered Marilyn's instructions not to doll herself up, and decided it would be best not to wear her riding hat.

If she was supposed to have ridden off in a hurry to find her cousin she would not have bothered about herself but would have run out of the house as she was.

What was more, the Marquis, if he noticed her at all, would think she looked very countrified, and certainly not smart like the ladies with whom he usually rode.

As she dressed she thought how much her father and mother would disapprove of her acting a lie even to please her cousin.

However, it was the first time Marilyn had asked her to do anything for her for a very long time, and

Hermia thought she must not only help her, but pray that if she was happy she would be much kinder to her and everybody else.

She had a feeling that Marilyn had changed a great deal since she grew up.

She was in fact becoming more and more like the Countess who always had something unpleasant to say, and looked down on most people as if they were dirt beneath her feet.

When Hermia was dressed and it was not much after six o'clock, she crept very softly down the stairs so that nobody should hear her.

Perhaps it was slightly reprehensible, but now that she had the chance of riding one of the fine horses from the Hall which she missed more and more every day, she did not want to ride straight to Bluebell Wood as Marilyn had instructed her to do, but to enjoy a good ride first while she had the opportunity.

When she reached the stable she found as she expected that, late in the evening, without their hearing him, a groom from the Hall had put a horse in one of the many empty stalls.

The previous Vicar must have been very much richer than her father because he had extended the stables, and there was room for a dozen horses or more.

Now there was only the Vicar's new yearling which was only partly broken in.

He was training it not only to draw the gig in which he made his rounds in the Parish, but also the old-fashioned but comfortable chaise in which he drove his wife and daughter.

Rufus, as they had named him, being a chestnut, was excellent for the work he had to do, but certainly looked outclassed by the horse in the next stall.

When she saw him Hermia felt her heart leap in excitement and she knew that for the next hour she was really going to enjoy herself as she had not been able to do for many a year.

She recognised the horse, for she had ridden him before, and knew he was called *Bracken*.

She patted him and made a fuss of him while she fetched her side-saddle which was hanging on the wall.

She was just tightening the girths when the old man who looked after her father's horse and worked in the large, untidy garden came shuffling through the stable-door.

"Be ye goin' ridin', Miss Hermia?" he asked. "Oi thinks as 'ow the 'orse had been sent for t'Reverend."

"No, I am riding this morning, Jake," Hermia replied, "and do not tell Papa, if you see him, that I have gone, as it is a secret."

Jake took sometime to digest this before he said:

"Oi'll keep me mouth shut, Miss Hermia, an' Oi 'spect ye'll enjoy yersel' wi' a fine animal loik 'e."

"I shall, Jake! It is a long time since I have had anything so magnificent to ride."

As she spoke Hermia led *Bracken* out of the stables and Jake held his bridle as she stepped onto a mounting-block.

She could manage to lift herself into the saddle without one, but she thought for Marilyn's sake that she should arrange her skirt tidily, although she was quite sure that whatever she did her cousin would find fault.

When she had settled herself in the saddle she smiled at Jake and said:

"Not a word now to anybody until I return!"

"Oi'll hold me tongue!" Jake promised and Hermia rode off.

She entered the Park and riding in the opposite direction from Bluebell Wood went past the wood nearest to the Vicarage which was marked on the maps as Brook Wood, but was known to everybody in the village as Witch Wood.

This was the wood in which they believed Satan's revels, which they whispered about amongst themselves, took place.

This morning Hermia was not interested in the woods but in wanting the horse under her to gallop as swiftly as it was possible for him to do.

On the other side of Witch Wood there was a level piece of ground she had always hoped her Uncle would make into a miniature race-course, such as a number of race-horse owners had built on their own estates.

But he had refused, saying he found it boring to visit the same place day after day.

"As I own 10,000 acres I have plenty of room to ride where I wish," he explained, "which is good for my horse as well as for me."

Now as Hermia saw the flat grassland which extended for over a mile she drew in her breath with excitement and gave *Bracken* his head.

When she slowed him down to a trot after the wild gallop they had both enjoyed to the full, she felt anything she had to do for Marilyn in payment for this delight, was well worthwhile.

She rode on, seeing parts of the estate she had known ever since she was a child, but had not been able to visit for a long time.

Then knowing time was passing and she must not

be late for Marilyn she rode *Bracken* back past Witch Wood and over the Park towards the wood where Marilyn would be riding with the Marquis.

Now Hermia had to go very much more slowly because the rabbit-holes were dangerous, and also because of the low branches on the trees.

It was warm as she had expected, getting warmer as the sun moved up the sky, and she was glad that she had not put on the jacket of her riding-habit.

Instead she was just wearing a white muslin blouse.

It was old and had been mended, darned and patched in places, but it was the best she had.

She thought once again that if the Marquis thought about her at all he would believe she had just come straight from the Bed-Room of the dying woman to fetch her cousin.

Now that the moment was upon her and she had to act the part that Marilyn had assigned to her, she rehearsed in her mind what she would say.

She hoped that if she spoke urgently and with a note of sincerity in her voice the story would be believed.

She entered the wood and moved slowly under the trees, along a path that led into the very centre of it.

The bluebells and primroses were over and the undergrowth was very much higher than it had been in the spring.

Occasionally Hermia would see the wild orchid called 'Lady's Slippers' growing under the trees, and there was also a profusion of small mushrooms which she had always believed showed where the fairies had danced the night before.

Because she could not help it she began to tell herself a fantasy story in which a Princess escaped from the goblins and was taken to safety by a wood-nymph.

She was just getting to the exciting part of the tale when she heard voices and realised that Marilyn and the Marquis were not far from her deep in the heart of the wood.

She drew in her breath, then having kicked her heel into *Bracken* to make him move faster she managed by the time she reached them to sound as if she was in a great hurry and almost breathless from the speed at which she had come.

Only when she had her first glimpse of Marilyn did she realise how untidy she herself must look.

Her hair had been blown about her forehead from the speed at which she had galloped, her cheeks were flushed, and although she was not aware of it her eyes were shining because it had all been so enjoyable.

Marilyn on the other hand, dressed in an exquisitely cut summer riding-habit of pale blue silk trimmed with white braid and with a jabot of lace at her chin, looked as if she had just stepped out of Rotten Row.

Her riding-hat was encircled with a gauze veil of the same colour as her habit and hung down her back.

As she turned to look at Hermia with well-simulated surprise her face was serene and lovely, and everything about her was neat and tidy to the zenith of perfection.

Hermia rode up to her at such a pace that she had to pull Bracken to a standstill so sharply that he reared up most effectively.

"Hermia!" Marilyn exclaimed. "What is the matter? Why are you here?"

"Oh, Marilyn, I have been looking for you everywhere!" Hermia replied. "Poor old Mrs. Burles is dying, but she says she cannot do so until she has said goodbye to you and thanked you for all your kindness to her."

Because she was feeling nervous Hermia had not attempted to alter the words that Marilyn had instructed her to say.

She thought as she said them, that they sounded somewhat contrived.

Marilyn gave a little cry that sounded very theatrical.

"Oh, poor Mrs. Burles!" she exclaimed. "Of course I must go to her!"

She turned her horse sharply as she spoke and passing Hermia gave it a sharp flick of the whip.

She had gone quite a way before as if she suddenly remembered what she had planned she turned her head to call out:

"Show His Lordship the way back to the Hall, and then follow me. I shall need you."

"I will do that," Hermia replied.

She thought as she spoke that Marilyn was making quite certain that she did not linger and ingratiate herself with the Marquis.

For the first time she looked at him.

He had turned his horse so that it was across the path, and now he was nearer to her than Hermia expected.

Then she gave an audible gasp and realised simultaneously that she had been very stupid.

She might have guessed that the man who had kissed her and given her a guinea for helping him would turn out to be the Marquis of Deverille.

He was looking, she thought, as he had the other day, very much like the Devil, except that as she met his eyes she realised there was a slight twinkle in them and a decided twist to his lips.

For the moment she could only stare at him, wondering wildly what she should say.

"So you are not a milk-maid after all!"

He spoke with that dry, drawling voice which he had used before.

Then as she felt the colour come flooding into her face, Hermia in a voice which did not sound like her own, replied:

"No, and you had no . . . right to . . . think I was!"

What she had meant was that he had no right to kiss her, and feeling shy and very embarrassed at meeting him again she could only wonder how she could make him realise how badly he had behaved.

"Do you want me to apologise?" the Marquis asked.

With an effort Hermia lifted her chin and looked at him defiantly.

"It is too late now for that! Were you able to find the Blacksmith without any . . . difficulty?"

"I rode back to where I was staying and left my grooms to cope with it."

"That is where you will wish to go now, and I will show you the way."

"There is no hurry. I am interested as to why at one moment you are pretending to be a milk-maid, and the next you appear as an Amazon on an exceedingly well-bred horse."

"I was not pretending to be a milk-maid!" Hermia retorted quickly. "And even if I were . . ."

She stopped because she thought what she was about to say would make the conversation even more embarrassing than it already was.

"What you are saying is that I had no right to kiss you," the Marquis said slowly. "Surely you must be aware that if you walk about alone looking as you do, you are a temptation to any man who sees you?"

"Not the sort of men I meet here in the country," Hermia replied, "but perhaps the Gentlemen who come from London have different ideas from ours about . . . respect and . . . propriety?"

She tried to speak defiantly, but because she was still feeling shy her voice sounded rather small, weak and ineffective.

"I stand rebuked!" the Marquis said and she knew he was laughing at her.

"If Your Lordship will ride on a little way," Hermia said, "I will show you a path which will lead you back into the Park. Then it will be easy for you to find your way to the Hall."

"I have already said," the Marquis replied, "I am in no hurry."

As his horse was across the path and the trees were close together it was impossible for her to go round him. Hermia could therefore only look at him help-lessly and wonder what she could do.

"Suppose you tell me who you are?" the Marquis asked. "And why you make it your business, besides collecting eggs, to fetch young women to the death-beds of the villagers?"

Again Hermia was certain he was mocking her, and she thought with a little flicker of anger that he was living up to his appearance.

"If you are interested," she said coldly, "my father is the Vicar of Little Brookfield, and when the old woman who is . . . dying asked for my . . . Cousin Marilyn

I . . . naturally came in . . . search of her."

"And you were aware this was where she would be?"

Hermia drew in her breath.

She knew it was a very pertinent question and something Marilyn should have foreseen he might ask.

After a very short pause she replied:

"I was going up to the . . . Hall when . . . somebody told me they had seen you . . . riding in this . . . direction."

She tried to make the lie sound convincing.

At the same time, because the Marquis was looking at her closely she stumbled a little over her words.

"So Marilyn is your cousin," the Marquis said slowly.

"Yes, as I have just told you," Hermia answered, "and she will be waiting for me. Please, My Lord, let me show you the way. Then I can hurry back to help her."

"Do you enjoy death-bed scenes?"

Again Hermia was aware he was mocking her, and now she was quite certain in her own mind that he did not believe that anybody was dying.

She hated him even more violently for being so perceptive and wanted to escape from him.

She had the feeling that his eyes, despite his drooping eye-lids, were sharp and penetrating and that he was well aware that she was becoming more and more involved in her lies and telling them very badly.

Then she hoped she was being needlessly apprehensive.

Yet because he was challenging her she wished that she could take him into the village and show him Mrs. Burles dying in her bed with Marilyn sitting beside her like an Angel of Mercy.

However, that being impossible she could only remain silent, her face turned away from him.

She was unaware that as she did so the sun flickering through the thick branches of the trees made her hair shine as if it were made of the same gold as the guinea he had pressed into her hand.

She was thinking of that, and of how he had insulted her, and also of the strange hardness and possessiveness of his lips when he kissed her.

Again as if he could read her thoughts he said:

"I appreciate that you are angry with me, and while I can only apologise again for mistaking your calling, I do not apologise for kissing you, because you are so unexpectedly beautiful!"

"It was an...intolerable way to...behave, My Lord, and I have no wish to...discuss it!"

"I imagine you have never been kissed before," the Marquis remarked reflectively.

"Of course not!" Hermia said angrily.

Then a sudden thought struck her and she turned her face towards him saying in a very different voice:

"Please...you will not tell...Marilyn or my uncle what...happened? If they spoke of it to Mama and Papa they would be very...upset."

There was something pathetic in the way she pleaded with him and after a moment the Marquis said:

"I have many faults, but I have never done anything so dishonourable as to talk about any woman I have kissed."

He saw the little sigh of relief Hermia gave and added quietly:

"Forget it! At the same time, because I am interested I would like to know what you did with the guinea I gave you."

"I wanted to throw it away!"

"But instead you kept it?"

"Certainly not! I put it in the poor-box. When Papa finds it he will be able to help a great number of people who at this moment are desperately in need of help."

"Why at this moment?"

Hermia looked at him in surprise.

"Surely you are aware of the suffering there is in the country as an aftermath of the war?"

He did not speak and she went on:

"The farmers are having a desperate time after the bad harvest of last year, and because of the cheap food which is coming into the country from the Continent. They cannot afford to take on more labourers, and with so many men coming out of the Services there is terrible unemployment."

She thought the Marquis looked at her in surprise and he certainly raised his dark eye-brows before he replied:

"I should have thought your Uncle was rich enough to see there was no unemployment on his estate."

Hermia was silent.

She knew that her Uncle had refused, despite her father's pleading, to take on a number of young men in the village who had either returned from the war or who were now grown up and required work.

In fact, they had had several angry arguments about it quite recently and the last time the Earl had roared at his brother:

"Whatever you think, I am not a Philanthropic Society, and the sooner you get that into your head the better."

Her father had come home very depressed and said:

"If only I could employ them all myself, but you know I cannot do that, and I hate to tell them I have failed to find them work."

"You have done your best, darling," her mother had said, "and no man could do more."

"I know, I know," her father replied, "but if I had the running of the estate, I could quite easily take on several dozen more men and give them work which would eventually pay for itself."

He had been depressed the whole evening, and it had taken her mother a long time to coax him back into his habitual good-humour.

Now it occurred to Hermia that if the Marquis was as rich as Marilyn had said he was, he could take on extra workmen on his estate and might even persuade her uncle to be more generous.

Without thinking, speaking in the same way as she talked to her father and mother as if she were their contemporary, she said:

"Surely you must be aware, as you too are a Land-lord, that if you developed new industries it would create work for men who otherwise would starve, or take to stealing."

"What sort of industries are you thinking of?"

Hermia was sure he was sneering at her behind the drawling words, yet because she was determined to make him understand she said:

"I have no idea of what your land is like, but here, for instance, if Uncle John would only listen, there is so much timber ready to be felled that he could employ at least two dozen workmen in a new Timber-Yard."

She knew the Marquis was listening and went on.

"There is also a gravel-pit which was not worked during the war which could be re-opened, and at the far end of the estate there is an ancient slate-quarry, and slate is always needed for the building of new houses."

"I see you are remarkably well informed," the Marquis remarked. "Are these your ideas or your father's?"

"They should be the ideas of great Landlords like yourself, My Lord," Hermia retorted.

Then because she felt it was a mistake to antagonise him she said:

"Please, if you get the chance, will you speak about such things to my Uncle? I feel sure he would listen to you, even though he will not listen to Papa."

"I very much doubt if he would listen to me," the Marquis replied, "but if I do what you ask, will you forgive me my sins?"

"I think, My Lord, it would be best not to talk about them, but to let me show you the way to the Hall."

She thought as she spoke that she had spent far more time with the Marquis than she should have done, and if Marilyn was aware of it she would be very angry.

"Please..." she said. "I must go to my cousin. She will be...expecting me."

"Very well," the Marquis said, "but before you ride ahead to show me the way suppose you tell me your name?"

"It is Hermia!"

"I imagine when you were christened your parents were thinking of you as a female version of the Messenger of the Gods!"

For the first time since they had been talking Hermia gave a little laugh.

"It is clever of you to be aware of that. Most people merely exclaim: 'What a funny name!' and expect me to be called 'Jane,' 'Anne,' 'Sarah,' or 'Mary.'"

"Why those names in particular?" the Marquis enquired curiously.

"Because they are what is considered suitable for a Vicar's daughter," Hermia replied demurely.

"You mean it would be very much out of character for your parents to be thinking of Olympus! Well, shall I tell you that at the moment you look much more like Persephone, leaving Hades to bring Spring back to the world."

He spoke in his dry, sarcastic voice which did not make his words sound like a compliment, but again Hermia laughed and it was a very happy, spontaneous sound.

"Why are you laughing?"

He had drawn his horse up beside her on the path and as he did so she glanced at him.

Then without thinking she was being impertinent she replied:

"You must be aware who I thought you were after you left me!"

"Oh, now I understand!" the Marquis said. "Very well, lead the Devil out of Hades!"

Hermia did not reply, but she thought Bluebell Wood was not her idea of Hades.

She was riding ahead of the Marquis and she thought that if Marilyn was ever aware she had lingered and talked with him for so long she would be very, very angry.

Only when they reached the footpath which led out of the wood into the Park did she hesitate for a moment.

She had intended to go back the way she had come through Bluebell Wood, but that, she knew, would take longer than if she rode into the Park with the Marquis.

While he went on to the Hall she would ride in the opposite direction towards the village.

She felt that he would not suggest accompanying her, but if he did she must try to find some excuse to prevent him from doing so.

As she made up her mind, she rode ahead, and a few minutes later they could see the Park in front of them and in the distance the Hall, looking very large and very impressive in the sunshine.

As the path came to an end Hermia drew *Bracken* to a standstill.

"You can find your way back from here, My Lord."

"I realise that," he replied, "and I should thank you for performing your task so efficiently."

The way he spoke made Hermia nervous that he was making it clear that he did not for one moment believe that she had summoned Marilyn to a death-bed.

Then she told herself she was being needlessly apprehensive.

Why should the Marquis not believe what he had been told? But even if he did, she had the feeling that it would not make him wish to marry Marilyn without having many other far better reasons for doing so.

He drew his horse alongside hers and sat looking at her with an expression on his face she did not understand.

It was as if he was appraising her in a manner that was vaguely insulting, and yet at the same time, because he was so cynical and bored, complimentary.

She did not know why she thought this, and yet she was sure it was true.

He did not move and after a moment Hermia said:

"Goodbye . . . My Lord!"

"Goodbye, Hermia!" the Marquis replied. "I shall be looking forward, as of course the Devil expected, to seeing you again."

Hermia smiled and he saw the dimples in her cheeks.

"As I am not Persephone," she said, "that is very unlikely, unless of course the gods have a special message for you, which is again unlikely."

She did not wait for his reply, but started *Bracken* moving quickly away from him, at the same time being careful of the rabbit-holes and the low boughs of the trees.

She did not look back, but she had the feeling the Marquis was watching her go.

Only when she had reached the very end of the path and was nearing the gate which would take her out onto the road leading to the village did she look back towards the Hall.

She could see him in the distance riding slowly across the top of the path and felt glad he had not followed her.

She rode out onto the dusty road and trotted home, thinking it would be a very long time before she had the chance of riding *Bracken* or any horse like him again.

At the same time it had been an exciting morning, and very different from the monotony of other mornings in which for months nothing unusual happened.

She put *Bracken* in the stable and Jake took off his bridle and saddle.

"If *Bracken* is not fetched before this evening,"

Hermia said, "I shall ride him again this afternoon."

"Ye do that, Miss Hermia," Jake agreed. "'t be a cryin' shame anyone rides as well as you do shouldn't 'ave a 'orse."

"I enjoyed myself this morning."

She reluctantly said goodbye to *Bracken* and left the stable to go into the house.

She was thinking quickly what she should say to her father and mother, and when she entered the Dining-Room where they were having breakfast her mother said:

"Nanny told me you went riding early this morning on a horse that came from the Hall. Surely that is a most unusual thing to happen?"

"Very unusual," Hermia agreed, kissing first her mother then her father, "but Marilyn wanted me to do something for her."

"Marilyn?" Mrs. Brooke exclaimed. "But you have not heard from her for months!"

Hermia sat down and started to eat a boiled egg which was waiting for her covered with a little woollen cap to keep it warm.

Instead of answering her mother she said to her father:

"Tell me, Papa, have you ever heard of the Marquis of Deverille?"

"Deverille?" her father replied. "Of course I have! 'Deverille the Devil' is famous in the sporting world."

Hermia stared at him in astonishment.

"What did you call him?" she asked.

"It is what they shout on the race-course when his horse wins," her father explained. "He is always said to have the Devil's own luck, so it is obvious that the racing crowd who never miss a trick should call him

'Deverille the Devil!'"

"That is exactly what he looks like!"

"I heard he was staying at the Hall," her father said. "When did you meet him?"

Hermia realised she had made a slip and said quickly:

"He was riding with Marilyn..."

"And she asked you to ride with them?" Mrs. Brooke asked with astonishment. "I cannot understand why she should do that!"

Hermia knew it was impossible to explain and she merely said:

"Marilyn came here yesterday, Mama, and she was very pleasant. She asked me to meet her this morning in the Bluebell Wood, and the Marquis was with her."

"I am astonished!" her mother answered. "Perhaps now, darling, they will ask you to the Hall."

Hermia knew this was very unlikely, but there was nothing she could reply except: "I hope so, Mama," and go on eating her egg.

"Deverille is an extraordinary chap!" her father remarked in a voice which told her he was following his own train of thought. "He is an exceptional rider. He is the foremost Corinthian in the 'Four-In-Hand Club,' and I have always heard that he is an exceptional pugilist besides other accomplishments. Yet he always looks as if he has lost a florin and found a fourpenny bit!"

"Do you mean he looks bored, Papa?"

"Exactly!" her father replied. "Bored and cynical. There have been a lot of cartoons done of him, and they always depict him looking like the Devil who is down on his luck!"

He laughed before he went on:

"That certainly is untrue to life. Deverille is rich, important and as we used to say at Oxford, 'riding high!' So there is nothing in his life to make him look so gloomy."

"There must be some reason for his attitude," Mrs. Brooke remarked.

"I heard John say once that he was crossed in love when he was a young man, and it turned him sour. I suppose if he is staying at the Hall the Countess has decided to try and marry him off to Marilyn."

"The Marquis does not sound as if he would make her happy," Hermia revealed.

She saw the expression on her father's face and knew he was thinking, as she did, that all the Countess was interested in was the position which Marilyn would occupy as the Marquis's wife.

Neither she nor the Earl would be concerned whether she would find him someone she could love and who would love her.

But it was not the sort of thing her father would say, and even while Hermia was sure he thought it, her mother gave a little sigh before she said:

"Perhaps once Marilyn is married your brother will allow Hermia to ride again. You know how she misses it."

"It was lovely riding this morning," Hermia said, "and I went for a long ride beyond Witch Wood before I joined Marilyn at the time she told me to."

"I am glad you enjoyed it, but you may be stiff tomorrow," her father said.

"If I am," Hermia replied, "Mama has concocted a new salve for stiff joints which all the village is begging her to give them."

"It is in such demand that I shall have to work for

hours to make enough," Mrs. Brooke said. "And that reminds me, was Mrs. Burles pleased with the cough mixture you took her?"

"I think she was, Mama," Hermia replied. "At the same time she is growing very old and senile. She went rambling on about her son Ben and is obviously very fussed about him."

"A regular ne'er-do-well," the Vicar exclaimed, "and not quite right in the head. At the same time, the boy is often hungry and nobody will give him any work when there are far better and stronger men in the village sitting about with idle hands."

He spoke bitterly and Hermia wished the Marquis could hear him and understand how depressing it was for strong and healthy men to be idle through no fault of their own.

"The trouble with Ben," Mrs. Brooke said in her soft voice, "is that he has never really grown up and he is into every sort of mischief that he can find. But of course that does not help his mother."

"She is very old," Hermia said. "Instead of giving her cough mixture, Mama, what she really needs is an elixir of youth!"

Mrs. Brooke did not laugh.

"I only wish I could find one! It is what half the people here in the village want, although I have a feeling if they had enough good food a lot of them would look twenty years younger in a few days."

"I spoke to John about it the day before yesterday," the Vicar said getting up from the table, "but as usual, he would not listen to me!"

There was a note of disappointment and frustration in his voice which made his wife watch him with anxious eyes as he went from the Dining-Room.

Then she said to Hermia:

"I know what I will do, darling! I will make up a bottle of my soothing syrup and you shall take it to Mrs. Burles. Perhaps that will make her feel a little better."

"She was very depressed, Mama," Hermia replied, "and I know she will be delighted with anything you give her and believe that every spoonful is full of magic. In other words you are a Witch!"

Mrs. Brooke laughed and Hermia said jokingly:

"You will have to be careful, Mama, that they do not become frightened of you as they were of the poor old woman who lived in Witch Wood."

"You surely are not old enough to remember Mrs. Wombatt?" Mrs. Brooke asked.

"I do not remember ever seeing her," Hermia answered, "but of course in the village they believe she still haunts the wood, and that Satan dances with her ghost as he used to dance with her when she was alive!"

"I have never heard such nonsense!" her mother said. "The poor old thing was about ninety when she died and too old to dance with anybody, let alone Satan!"

"They make it sound exciting when they tell me stories of how when she cursed people they withered away or some terrible accident happened to them, or when she gave them one of her magic charms everything went right."

"Then I wish she could give you one," Mrs. Brooke smiled. "For I would love you, my darling, to have a magical horse, some magical gowns, and a wonderful magical Ball at which everybody would admire you!"

"Thank you, Mama, that is just what I want for myself," Hermia said, "and if I tell myself stories in which all that happens, perhaps it will come true."

She was laughing as she carried the empty plates from the Dining-Room into the kitchen and she did not see the look of pain on her mother's face.

Mrs. Brooke knew that loving and sweet though her daughter was, there was nothing for her in the future except a very restricted life in Little Brookfield.

She was barred from the parties which took place at the Hall and even from riding her Uncle's horses.

"It is not fair!" Mrs. Brooke said to herself.

Then because she could never be parted long from the husband she loved so deeply, she hurried from the Dining-Room to find him in the small Study where he had started work on the sermon he would preach on Sunday to the few villagers who came to Church to listen to him.

chapter four

RELUCTANTLY Hermia walked towards Mrs. Burles'
cottage which was at the end of the village carrying
the tonic her mother had made.

She always found Mrs. Burles exhausting.

Sometimes she was more or less sensible, but at
other times her mind wandered and she talked on and
on, really not making sense.

There had been quite a lot of things to do in the
house after luncheon, and Hermia had then hurried to
the stables to see if there was a chance of having one
more ride on *Bracken*.

To her disappointment he had already gone and she
realised that one of the grooms must have come while
they were having their meal and taken him home.

For a moment she felt her disappointment turn to
anger that she should have been deprived of something
she wanted so much.

Then she told herself that she was very lucky to

have been able to ride this morning, and it was greedy to expect to have the same joy again in the afternoon.

She also suspected that Marilyn might have realised how long she had talked to the Marquis and had deliberately sent for *Bracken* to punish her.

Then she told herself that once again she was being over-imaginative and Marilyn could have no idea that she had not hurried after her immediately as she had been told to do.

At the same time she did not regret it.

It had been exciting to talk to somebody like the Marquis, even though she hated him.

He might look cynical, he might behave in what she thought was a very reprehensible manner. Nevertheless he was obviously intelligent and she thought he was without exception one of the smartest men she had ever seen or could imagine.

The way he held himself, the way he sat his horse, and the almost blinding shine of his polished boots was something, she thought, which would colour her fantasy stories in the future, even though she cast him in the role of the villain.

She found herself thinking of him all the time she was walking towards Mrs. Burles' cottage.

When she was within sight of it she saw Ben Burles come running out of the low door.

He looked down the road and she thought he must have seen her, because he scuttled off in the opposite direction in a surreptitious manner as if he had something to hide.

'I expect he is up to some mischief,' she thought, thinking of her father's words.

She reached the cottage door and knocked loudly because Mrs. Burles was inclined to be deaf.

It took sometime for her to rise out of the armchair in which she habitually sat in front of the stove and come to the door.

She opened it a few inches, peered round it to see who was standing there, then said:

"Come in, Miss, come in! Oi were hopin' ye'd remember Oi were in pain, an' a real pain it be!"

Hermia entered the cottage, thinking as she had often thought before that it needed a lot of repair. It was something her Uncle should order to be done for his tenants even though they paid only a shilling or two a week.

She knew her father had spoken about the state of the cottages and had told his brother that many of those occupied by aged pensioners leaked when it rained.

The Earl had replied that he had no money to waste on a lot of old people, especially those who had sons who could do the repairs themselves.

The room however was clean, and as Mrs. Burles lowered herself very carefully into the armchair Hermia sat down in a high-backed one near her so that she could hear what she had to say.

"I have brought you a tonic to make you better," she said. "My mother says you are to take a spoonful every morning, one after your midday meal, and one when you go to bed at night."

"It be good of ye, Miss, very good," Mrs. Burles said. "Oi needs somethin', not only fer me body, but fer me mind."

"This will soon make you feel better," Hermia said optimistically.

"It's worried Oi be, worried all the time, an' Ben shouldn't do it, he shouldn't!"

"Do what?" Hermia asked curiously.

"She'll cast a spell on 'e, she will," Mrs. Burles went on as though Hermia had not spoke. "Oi've warned 'e, time after time, not to go near that old Witch, but 'e'll never listen to me!"

Hermia realised she was talking of old Mrs. Wombatt, who used to live in Witch Wood, and who the villagers still believed haunted it.

Because she could see Mrs. Burles' puckered face and the fear in her eyes, she leaned forward to put her hand on the old woman's and said quietly:

"Listen, Mrs. Burles, Mrs. Wombatt is dead. She has been dead for a long time, and she cannot hurt anybody now, so that you need not be afraid for Ben."

"She'll put a curse on 'e!" Mrs. Burles repeated. "He's no right to go there, as Oi tells him. An' they says that Satan heself has been seen with her."

The way she spoke told Hermia there was no use arguing.

This was one of her bad days, and she knew that Mrs. Burles would never believe that not only the poor old woman who had lived in Witch Wood was dead, but her magic had died with her.

She was quite certain that if Mrs. Wombatt had been a Witch, she was a White one.

Hermia thought she had magic powers because she had used herbs when she cooked, had told the fortunes of the village girls, and had given the older folk cures for rheumatism and colic which they believed healed them.

'It is no use arguing with her about a woman who has been dead for such a long time,' Hermia thought.

Instead she went to the table, found a spoon and poured a little of her mother's tonic into it.

"Swallow this," she said to Mrs. Burles, "and you will soon feel better, and I am sure it will help you to sleep."

She knew her mother had added camomile and a little verlain to the other herbs the tonic contained. Although she disapproved of giving those who were hale and hearty any form of sedative, it was different for those who were very old and whose minds wandered.

The old woman swallowed what was in the spoon and said:

"That be good! Give Oi some more."

"No, that is enough for the moment," Hermia said, "but you must remember to take another spoonful before you go to bed."

She put the tonic in the centre of the table and said:

"Goodbye, Mrs. Burles. I know you would like me to thank my mother for what she has sent you."

She walked towards the door as she spoke and as she reached it Mrs. Burles said:

"Ye'll not tell Ben Oi talked to ye? He said everythin' he tells Oi be a secret."

"No, of course not," Hermia said soothingly. "Shut your eyes and forget about him. I expect he will be back soon to look after you."

Mrs. Burles did not seem to understand, and as Hermia opened the door she heard the old woman mutter to herself:

"'E shouldn't have gone there! Oi says to him, Oi says: 'Her'll curse ye, that's what her'll do!'"

'Poor old thing, she really gets madder and madder!' Hermia thought as she walked back through the village.

By now the sun had lost its heat and she longed to

ride as she had done in the past over the fields and through the woods just as the birds were going to roost.

It had been an enchantment when the last rays of the sun made the tree trunks look like burnished brass, and the shadows seemed full of mystery which increased as the dusk came bringing with it the night.

'Now that I have to walk it is not the same,' she thought, 'but I suppose it is better than nothing.'

There were so many parts of the estate that she now never saw and yet she could conjure them up like pictures in her mind and knew their beauty could never be forgotten.

When she was nearly home she found herself again thinking of the strange conversation she had had with the Marquis.

He might be cynical and sarcastic, but her father had said how successful he was on the race-course and always won the big races.

"That means he will be at Royal Ascot next week," Hermia told herself, remembering it started on Monday.

Because her father was interested in horses he always read the racing news in *The Morning Post* which was the only newspaper they had at the Vicarage, and in fact, the only one they could afford.

When Peter was at home they would have long discussions on the merits of the horses they read about.

After Peter had been to the Derby with some of his friends he had described to his father exactly what had happened and how thrilling it had been.

"What is more," he said boastfully, "I won £5!"

"You might have lost it," the Vicar replied warningly.

"I know, Papa, and I was very nervous that might happen," Peter said honestly. "However I won, and that paid all my expenses for the day and left me a little in hand."

His father smiled as if he understood what a satisfaction it had been.

From the way he talked Hermia was sure her father would have liked to be at Epsom with Peter, and she wondered if her brother would have the chance of going to Ascot.

It must be very frustrating for him, she thought, to know that his rich friends could afford to attend all the race-meetings, either travelling from Oxford for the day, or staying the night with some generous host or if they had no invitation, at an Hotel which was invariably very expensive.

And yet Peter, although she felt sorry for him, was seeing a great deal more of life than she was.

She wondered if there would ever be a chance of her going to a race-meeting, attending one of the Balls which took place after every big meeting, or even just travelling to London to see the shops.

Then she laughed.

Those things were out of reach so it was no use troubling about them.

"'If wishes were horses, beggars could ride,'" she quoted to herself and hurried into the Vicarage to tell her mother about Mrs. Burles.

*   *   *

They had waited for the Vicar for nearly a quarter-of-an-hour and Nanny was complaining crossly that her food was getting spoilt, when the Vicar arrived home.

Hermia heard old Jake taking the gig round to the stables, and when she opened the front door and her father came in to the hall, her mother came hurrying out of the Sitting-Room to exclaim:

"Darling, I have been so worried! What kept you so long?"

The Vicar kissed his wife affectionately and said:

"I have told you not to worry. As a matter of fact I would have been home in plenty of time if I had not been delayed when I reached the village."

"The village?" Hermia exclaimed. "What has happened in the village?"

As if the Vicar was aware he ought not to keep Nanny waiting any longer he walked into the Dining-Room and sat down at the head of the table.

"You will hardly believe what has happened," he said, "in fact, I do not believe it myself."

"What is it?" Mrs. Brooke asked.

"The Marquis of Deverille has disappeared!"

Hermia stared at her father as if she felt she could not have heard correctly what he said.

"What do you mean disappeared, Papa?"

"Exactly what I say," the Vicar replied. "The whole village is agog with it. Apparently everybody on the estate is out looking for him."

Hermia's eyes were very wide in her face, but it was her mother who exclaimed:

"Tell us everything, darling, from the beginning. I am trying to understand what you are saying."

"I find it difficult to understand it myself!" the Vicar said. "But when I was coming home half-a-dozen people stopped me all chattering like parrots."

He smiled before he went on:

"Before I could stop them from all talking at once, half the village was clustered round the gig."

He stopped speaking to help first his wife, then his daughter from the soup tureen that Nanny had put in front of him on the table.

It was a soup made with celery which always tasted delicious and was in fact, one of the Vicar's favourites.

He filled his own plate, then as he drank a spoonful Hermia begged:

"Please go on, Papa. We must know what happened!"

"Yes, of course," the Vicar replied. "Well, it appears that immediately after luncheon at the Hall my brother had arranged to take the Marquis to see his yearlings which he has in a field on the North side of the Park."

Hermia knew where this was, but she did not interrupt as her father went on:

"The two Gentlemen were apparently not hurrying themselves but talking as they rode when a groom came galloping after them to say that a visitor had arrived at the Hall asking to see the Earl urgently and saying that he could not wait."

The Vicar paused and took another spoonful of soup before he continued:

"My brother was obviously annoyed at having to go back, but as they had not gone very far he told the Marquis to go on alone. He then rode back to the Hall."

"Who did he find waiting for him?" Mrs. Brooke asked.

"The village did not seem to know this," the Vicar replied, "but they say that John was only a few minutes at the house before he rode off again to catch the Marquis up."

"Then what . . . happened?" Hermia asked breathlessly.

"He could not find him!"

"What do you mean—could not find him?" Mrs. Brooke enquired.

"Exactly what I say," her husband answered. "There was no sign of the Marquis and at a loss to understand what could have happened, John rode back to the stables."

He paused dramatically, almost as if he enjoyed keeping his audience in suspense as he drank some more soup.

"My brother had only just arrived in the stables when to his consternation the horse the Marquis had been riding came galloping in, his stirrups flapping at his sides, and his saddle empty!"

Hermia gave a little gasp.

"I thought he was a good rider!"

"He is!" the Vicar said. "In fact I have always been told that the Marquis has boasted that the horse has never been bred that can throw him!"

"On this occasion he must have been thrown!" Mrs. Brooke exclaimed.

"That of course, is what I gather John and everybody else thought," the Vicar said.

"What happened then?" Hermia asked.

"Naturally your Uncle told all the grooms to get mounted and find the Marquis as quickly as possible."

There was a little pause before Mrs. Brooke asked:

"Are you saying that they have not found him?"

"There is no sign of him!" her husband replied.

"That is impossible!" Hermia exclaimed. "He must be somewhere not very far away!"

The Vicar finished his soup and as Nanny took away the tureen and came back with the next course he said:

"As soon as I have finished eating I am going up to the Hall to see if I can help in any way. According to Wade, who is a sensible man, everybody on the estate has been searching all the afternoon and evening, but there is not a sign of the Marquis anywhere."

Hermia and her mother both knew that Wade was the Head Keeper and had been at the Hall for many years.

He was a man who did not speak much, but what he said could be believed and they could understand that the mystery of the Marquis's disappearance was, if Wade had said so, unexaggerated.

"Yes, of course you must go to see if you can help, darling," Mrs. Brooke said, "but it does seem incredible that they cannot find him."

"I quite agree with you, but Wade told me they have searched everywhere."

He smiled as he added:

"It is a pity his horse cannot talk, because he in fact, must know where he left his distinguished rider."

Hermia was silent.

It flashed through her mind that perhaps after all, as she had thought the first time she met him, the Marquis was the Devil and he had now returned to the Underworld from which he came and they would never see him again.

"I should have thought the only thing any of us

can do," Mrs. Brooke replied, "is somehow to find the Marquis."

"Well, for one place he is not here in the Vicarage!" her husband said.

He put his arms around his wife and held her close against him as he said:

"I was looking forward to our having a quiet evening, but I will not be any longer than I can help. I suppose it would be a mistake for me to take Hermia with me?"

"She had better stay with me," Mrs. Brooke replied.

Hermia knew that her mother was thinking that if, as she suspected, the Marquis was being thought of as a suitable husband for Marilyn, they would certainly not want her.

After her father had left, Hermia and her mother sat in the Sitting-Room discussing what could have happened. Then Mrs. Brooke said:

"You must have spoken to the Marquis this morning when he was with Marilyn. What is he like?"

"The best way I can describe him, Mama, is bored, cynical and very sarcastic!"

Mrs. Brooke looked surprised.

"Why should he be like that?"

"I expect he has been spoilt, Mama, through being so successful at everything he undertakes."

"Do you think that Marilyn is in love with him?" her mother enquired.

"She is very anxious to marry him, Mama, and of course it is something that would please Aunt Edith."

"Of course," her mother agreed, and there was no need for Hermia to explain herself any further.

It was nearly eleven o'clock when her father returned, and as he came into the hall his wife and daughter sprang to their feet eagerly.

"Is there any news, Papa?" Hermia asked before her mother could speak.

"None at all," the Vicar said. "It seems quite inexplicable, and I have never known John to be so agitated."

"And Edith?" Mrs. Brooke enquired.

"She had no time for me, as you can imagine," the Vicar replied, "and I was informed that Marilyn is so distressed that she has taken to her bed."

"I must say it is a terrible thing to happen when one is entertaining a guest, whoever he may be," Mrs. Brooke remarked. "I suppose there is nothing we can do to help?"

"Nothing," the Vicar replied, "except pray he has not been murdered for any money he might have been carrying."

He paused before he said:

"I suppose I should not tell you this, but John is sure this could be the work of the Marquis's heir presumptive—Roxford de Ville."

"What a strange name!" Hermia muttered.

Her father sat down in his usual chair near the fireplace.

"De Ville is spelt the French way and is his family name," he explained. "I believe they originally came from Normandy at the time of William the Conqueror."

"And you think that this man Roxford de Ville has murdered the Marquis?" Mrs. Brooke asked with an incredulous note in her voice.

"Personally I cannot believe it," the Vicar answered. "It would be too obvious. But there is no doubt, according to John, that there is a great deal of animosity between the two of them. The Marquis has paid de Ville's debts dozens of time and recently refused to do any more for him."

"So if he disposes of the Marquis he will inherit the title and his fortune?" Hermia asked.

"If he is not arrested for murder and hanged for it," her father replied.

"But surely if he was bound to be the chief suspect, that would be a very silly thing to do?" Hermia persisted.

"You are quite right, my dearest," her father agreed, "and that is why I do not believe the Marquis has been murdered. He must have fallen somewhere and so far they have not been able to find him. John will be sending everybody out to search for him again as soon as it is dawn."

He rose from his chair as he spoke saying:

"I imagine I shall be expected to go with them, so I am now going to bed, and thank you, my darlings, for waiting up for me."

They all went up the stairs together and Hermia kissed her father and mother an affectionate goodnight and went to her own bedroom.

It was small but her mother had made it very pretty, and she had around her all her special treasures which she had collected ever since she had been a child.

Some of the china ornaments had been given to her by Marilyn, and as she looked at them she thought she was sorry for her cousin.

"She must be anxious that she may have lost the man she wants to marry," Hermia murmured.

At the same time some intuition that she could not

deny told her that the Marquis had had no intention of marrying Marilyn, and was quite aware that she was trying to trick him into proposing to her.

She did not know how she knew this, but it was just as clear to her as if somebody had proved to her that was the truth.

'Poor Marilyn,' she thought sympathetically, 'she will be very disappointed. But doubtless when she is in London and looking so pretty there will be heaps of other men to offer her marriage.'

They might not be as important or as rich as the Marquis, but there was every chance that she would be happier with a man who was not so contemptuous of everything in life.

Hermia got into bed having pulled back the curtains from the window before she did so, and lay watching the stars come out and the moon creeping up the sky.

The moon was full, and she remembered that the villagers thought that was the time of the Witches' Sabbath, when they flew towards it on their broomsticks.

The moment she thought of it she imagined she could see one silhouetted for a moment against the moon overhead.

Then suddenly she gave a little cry and sat up in bed.

If her uncle was right and the Marquis's wicked heir had murdered him, she knew where those who were employed to do anything so evil would have hidden the body.

Nobody who lived in the village and on the estate would, she knew, dare to search old Mrs. Wombatt's cottage which was situated in the centre of Witch Wood.

They were so frightened of their own tales about it that they believed that although she was dead and buried her ghost haunted the place where she had lived.

That was more, on moonlit nights she could still be seen revelling with Satan.

Even somebody as sensible as Wade the Head Keeper would not go near the cottage in the wood.

"That is where he will be!" Hermia told herself.

Although she was so sure she was right, she knew that she would have to find out for certain.

She thought perhaps she should tell her father, but if she did so he would insist on coming with her, and she would look very silly if she was proved wrong. He might then question her as to why she was so interested in the Marquis.

It would be much easier to suggest in the morning that he should look there.

But for some reason Hermia could not explain to herself she felt she must look for him now, at this moment, and it was important not to wait.

She got out of bed and dressed herself, putting on the first gown that came to hand.

She tied back her hair with a bow of ribbon, and slipped round her shoulders a little woollen shawl in case she felt cold when she got outside.

In fact, that was unlikely because it had been so hot all day, and now it was still warm and there was no wind.

When she was ready Hermia very cautiously opened the door of her bedroom and crept down the stairs in her stockinged feet holding her shoes in her hands.

She let herself out through the kitchen-door at the back, so that she would not be heard by her father and mother who slept in the big Bed-Room over-looking the front of the house.

Putting on her shoes she started to walk through the garden which adjoined the main road where she was out of sight of the windows.

It was not likely that anybody would see her.

At the same time she knew that Nanny as well as her father and mother would have been astonished had they known she was walking about at this time of the night.

There was no need to use one of the entrances which led into her Uncle's Park.

Instead, as she had done often before, she climbed over the wall and dropping down onto the soft ground started off in the direction of Witch Wood.

The wood was the nearest one to the village which was why, Hermia thought, all those years ago Mrs. Wombatt had built herself a house there.

It had been in her grandfather's time, who from all she had heard had been very much like her father, good-natured and kind to everyone who lived on his land.

He had made no objection when Mrs. Wombatt, with the help of two young men she had bewitched, built a house partly of bricks, partly with the trunks of trees, and lived there alone.

Now as Hermia entered the lower end of Witch Wood she wondered if the tales the villagers told were true.

Perhaps in the moonlight she would see strange sights and hear the music to which the Witches danced echoing among the trees.

Then she told herself that even if they were there they would not hurt her, while the elves and fairies who had been her friends ever since she first learnt about them would protect her from coming to any harm.

The wood itself was very beautiful in the moon-light, and it was impossible to believe that any evil could mar such loveliness.

The moon shone silver through the branches of the trees and made strange patterns on the path along which Hermia walked.

She could see the stars brilliant as diamonds in the heavens above her, and if there was music it came from her heart and from the trees.

She had always believed as a little girl that if she listened against the trunk of a tree she would hear it breathing, and sometimes singing a little song to itself.

Any other sounds she imagined were made by the goblins who lived under the roots or by the squirrels who built their nests high up in its branches and were afraid of nothing except human beings.

It was a long way to the centre of the wood, but even as she drew nearer to Mrs. Wombatt's cottage she was not afraid.

She saw first the forest pool in which she knew the old woman had washed, and also drank the water.

It was a very beautiful pool surrounded by irises and kingcups and the still surface of the water looked in the moonlight as if it held mystical secrets.

Then just beyond it, half-hidden by the bushes that had grown up over the years, she saw Mrs. Wombatt's house.

It was in surprisingly good repair considering it had not been lived in for so long. The roof was intact and the chimney was still there.

Then as she reached it Hermia could see quite clearly

that the two small windows on each side of the door had been boarded up and she wondered who had taken the trouble to do this.

She stood looking at them, thinking that somebody who had not been afraid of the Witch's Curse must have come here since her death and protected the house against intruders.

There were not likely to be any, and she could only imagine it had been done on her Uncle's instructions, then thought that was unlikely.

She was quite sure, knowing him, that he would merely say that as far as he was concerned the house could fall down, and the sooner the better.

Then because the same instinct which had brought her here told her now she must look inside, she put out her hands towards a heavy wooden bar that lay across the centre of the door.

It was lodged firmly into two iron cradles, which looked, although it was difficult to see clearly, as if they had been added recently.

The bar of wood was heavy and it took all Hermia's strength to lift it, but she managed at last to do so, and dropped it onto the ground.

Then as she was ready to pull the door open she felt for the first time, afraid.

Suppose she found something horrible inside?

She felt a tremor of fear strike through her. Then as she trembled, she heard the soft hoot of an owl in one of the trees.

It was such a familiar sound and so much part of her life that it was reassuring, just as if her father or somebody she trusted was with her.

If the creatures of the forest were not afraid, then she had nothing to fear either.

She half opened the door and for a moment she could see nothing.

Then as her eyes grew accustomed to the darkness she could see something lying on the floor in the centre of the small room.

At first she thought it was just a pile of clothing, or perhaps some leaves.

Then her intuition told her it was a man and she knew that she had found the Marquis.

She opened the door as wide as it would go, and now the moonlight made it easy to see she was not mistaken.

There was a man's body lying still on the floor, and the first thing Hermia saw was the shine of his boots and then the white of his breeches.

She knelt down beside him, thinking with a sudden constriction of her heart that he was dead.

But as she put her hand on his forehead, feeling for it rather than seeing exactly where it was, she knew he was alive but unconscious.

To be quite certain she was not mistaken, she undid the buttons of his waist-coat and put her hand inside to feel his heart.

Through his fine linen shirt she could feel it beating faintly and now as she began to see more clearly in the darkness she saw his eyes were closed and there was blood on his forehead and on the side of his cheek.

It flashed through her mind that he had fought against those who must have brought him here!

Perhaps finally they had either shot him, or hit him with something heavy which had rendered him unconscious as he was now.

She took her hand from his heart and very gently felt his head.

She thought there was blood congealed in his hair and she was certain, although she dared not investigate further, that there was an open wound where he had been hit perhaps with a blunderbuss or a heavy stick.

'I must go and fetch help,' she thought.

Then as she would have risen to her feet the Marquis opened his eyes.

As he did so he made a movement with his hands and she was aware that he was struggling back to reality.

"What—has—happened?" he asked.

"You are all right and quite safe," Hermia replied, "but I think somebody has struck you on the head."

She was not certain if he had understood or not, but he made an effort as though he would sit up and she helped him.

She realised as she did so how big and heavy he was, but somehow she managed to assist him into a sitting position.

He groaned and tried to put his hand up to his forehead as if he felt dizzy.

"You are all right," she said again, "but I want, if possible, to get you away from here."

She had a sudden fear that whoever had brought him to the Witch's house and flung him down on the ground might return to finish him off, or to make sure he was still imprisoned and nobody had rescued him.

Now as he was sitting up she could see that the sleeve of his riding-jacket had been torn away from the shoulder and his cravat was untied and crumpled.

She looked at the hand he was attempting to put to his forehead and saw that the knuckles of his fingers were bleeding.

It was obvious he had put up a tremendous fight

against his assailants, whoever they were, but the blow from a heavy weapon was what had finally defeated him.

She let him rest for a moment. Then she said softly:

"Will you try to get to your feet while I help you? I do not want to leave you here alone while I fetch help."

The Marquis did not reply but she felt he understood what she had said to him, for he reached out his hand to try to find something by which he could pull himself up to his feet.

Putting her hand under his arm and straining every muscle in her body to assist him, Hermia thought it was only by a miracle and what she knew was his indomitable willpower that finally he stood upright.

She placed one of his arms over her shoulder so that he could use her as a crutch, and put her other arm round his waist.

Then step by step, afraid every moment he would fall down, she got him to the doorway.

She put her free hand up to prevent him from hitting his head on the lintel of the door, and he winced as if the part of his head that had been struck felt very tender.

But still he did not speak.

Then they were outside in the moonlight and moving at a snail's pace down the path by which she had come through the wood.

*   *   *

Afterwards Hermia asked herself how she had ever managed to take the Marquis so far, when she had all his weight leaning on her and only by directing his every step was she able to keep him on the path.

She felt at times he must have shut his eyes and just let her lead him as if he were blind.

Because of the way she was supporting him, she could not look at his face, but could only drag him to safety, knowing that if the men who had left him imprisoned in the cottage returned there was nothing she could do to save him.

It must have been over an hour before they reached the point in the wall where she had climbed into the Park.

There they stopped and when at last she was able to look up at the Marquis he collapsed onto the ground.

As she released her hold on him he lay stretched out with his eyes closed, and once again for one terrifying moment she felt he might be dead.

Then she knew he had just willed himself to follow her lead and was now too utterly exhausted to go on any further.

She felt very much the same herself, but she knew it would be easier now to fetch her father and it was also unlikely that anybody who was looking for the Marquis would find him here while she hurried home.

She climbed over the wall, feeling that the Marquis's weight on her had left her almost crippled.

But because she was frightened that he might disappear again while she was gone, she ran back the way she had come through the overgrown garden to the kitchen-door.

Inside the house she hurried up the stairs and without knocking burst into her parents' room.

They were both asleep, and as Hermia stood there gasping for breath her mother awoke first to ask:

"What is it, darling? What is the matter?"

"P–Papa...I want Papa!" Hermia gasped in a voice that did not sound like her own.

Her father sat up.

"What has happened? Who wants me?"

"I...I have found the...Marquis!"

For no reason she could understand tears began to run down her cheeks as she spoke.

"You have found the Marquis?" the Vicar repeated in astonishment. "Where was he?"

"He was in...Witch Wood, Papa, and I have...brought him...along the path as far as the wall...but he is badly...injured."

"In Witch Wood?" her father said. "I cannot understand why he should be there."

"He was put there by men who must have...attacked him. He has been hit on the head...but he is...alive!"

As if her father understood the urgency of what she was saying he started to get out of bed.

"Go and fetch Nanny," her mother said, "while Papa and I dress. If His Lordship is wounded, tell her we shall need hot water and bandages."

Hermia disappeared to do what she was told and by the time she had woken Nanny and explained what had happened her father was coming down the stairs.

"Show me where you have left him," he said. "I suppose I can manage to bring him back on my own?"

For the first time Hermia smiled.

"I brought him from the Witch's house to the wall."

"Obviously by magic," her father replied, "but I shall have to manage by more human means!"

They both laughed, then Hermia was running ahead of her father back to where she had left the Marquis.

It took both of them to carry him back through the Park gates and into the Vicarage.

He was unconscious and Hermia thought afterwards it was only because her father was so strong that with her help he could manage.

By the time they arrived at the Vicarage her mother and Nanny had made up the bed in Peter's room.

They also had the kettle boiling, fresh bandages ready torn from old sheets, and her mother's salves made from herbs and honey to treat the Marquis's wounds.

Hermia was sent away while they undressed him and got him into bed.

Then when she was allowed to see him he looked very different from how he had appeared to her before.

Wearing one of her father's nightshirts, with his eyes closed and a bandage round his head, he looked very much younger and neither cynical nor bored.

He might in fact have been one of Peter's contemporaries.

Looking down at him Hermia thought he was not the grand, much-acclaimed Marquis, but merely a young man who had been hurt and who would doubtless tomorrow suffer a great deal of pain.

"There is nothing more we can do for him tonight," she heard her mother say.

"Then you go to bed, my darling," her father answered, "and I will sit up with His Lordship in case he wakes. As soon as it is light I will go to the Hall, send a groom for the Doctor, and tell John that his visitor is safe, but somewhat the worse for wear!"

Mrs. Brooke moved towards the armchair—an old and dilapidated one—and put on it a spare pillow which she had taken from the bed and she arranged it so that her husband could rest his head.

"I will get a stool for your feet," she said, "and a

blanket to cover you. I do not expect he will recover consciousness for several hours."

"You are spoiling me," the Vicar teased.

"You know I hate you to be uncomfortable, darling," his wife replied, "and as I have a feeling that tomorrow will be a busy day, you will need all the sleep you can get."

"You are quite right, as you always are," the Vicar said. "I will fetch the stool. Where is it?"

"In front of my dressing-table, where it always is!"

The Vicar smiled as he went into the next room to fetch it.

Her mother put her arm around Hermia's shoulders.

"What made you look in old Mrs. Wombatt's house?" she asked.

"I was quite sure no one would dare to look for him there," Hermia replied, "and something told me that that was where the men who had attacked him would hide his body."

As she spoke she gave a little cry.

"Mama!" she exclaimed. "I know now who told them where to hide the Marquis!"

As she spoke Mrs. Burles' conversation came back to her.

"It was Ben!" she said aloud. "Ben knew that no one in the village would go into the Witch's cottage for fear of being cursed!"

She was quite certain this was true and she added:

"But why should Ben be involved in this? And why should the Marquis be attacked in such a horrible manner, even if Papa is right, and it was his heir who hates him?"

"I do not understand it either," her mother replied,

"but if you are right and Ben is mixed up in this it will not only get him into trouble, but will make things very uncomfortable for your Uncle John because one of his people is involved."

"Perhaps I had better say nothing about it."

"I think that would be wise, dearest," her mother answered, "at least until the Marquis himself can tell us what happened."

"Yes, of course, Mama, the best thing we can do is to wait," Hermia agreed.

She kissed her mother and went to her own room.

She thought as she undressed, her arms and shoulders aching from the weight of the Marquis's body, that tomorrow they would be able to learn the truth of the whole mystery.

In a way it would be very exciting.

Then she realised that when Marilyn learnt that the Marquis was in the Vicarage and that she had saved him she would be very angry.

"It is not my fault!" Hermia said aloud, as if Marilyn was accusing her.

Then she could almost see the anger in her cousin's eyes, and knew that whatever she might say in her own defense she would not be forgiven for interfering.

chapter five

IT was strange, Hermia thought, what a difference it had made to the Vicarage having the Marquis there.

For two days he lay unconscious, only occasionally murmuring nonsense and turning restlessly from side to side.

The Doctor, who was an old friend and came from the nearby market town, said:

"Let him rest, and Mrs. Brooke's magic potions are far better than anything I can prescribe."

He laughed as he spoke and Hermia was aware that her mothers fame for the herbs and natural ingredients she put together to cure almost every ill had spread all over the County.

He confirmed what Hermia already suspected, that the Marquis had fought violently against his assailants, only succumbing when they had hit him on the head with a heavy stick or perhaps a piece of wood.

Her mother's salve and the skilful way she bandaged him ensured that every day the wound got better.

That also applied to the Marquis's broken knuckles, the huge bruises on his body and, as the Doctor suspected, a fractured rib.

The Marquis's valet had come from the Hall, and although Nanny had exclaimed disagreeably that if they housed any more people the house would burst at the seams, Hickson had proved to be a real asset.

As he had the same original but somewhat caustic outlook on life as Nanny they got on famously.

He also demanded things for his master which neither the Vicar nor his wife would have thought of asking for and could not afford.

Legs of lamb, beef steaks, chickens and fat pigeons came into the house every day.

Although the Marquis at first could not eat them, Hermia thought even her father looked less harassed and her mother more beautiful because the food they were eating was so good.

Mrs. Brooke had at first remonstrated with Hickson saying:

"I cannot accept all these things from the Hall."

"Now you leave it to me, Ma'am," Hickson replied. "It's what 'Is Lordship's used to, 'an if 'e was a—stayin' there 'e'd have the best."

Mrs. Brooke knew this was true and when Hermia saw the huge peaches from the greenhouse and large bunches of Muscat grapes, she thought the Earl might occasionally have remembered how poor his brother was.

Her uncle came in and out of the Vicarage like a fussy hen who had lost a particularly prized chick.

Hermia suspected that it was Marilyn who urged her father to insist that the Marquis came back to the Hall, but when he recovered enough to think and talk he refused point-blank to be moved.

"I am very comfortable here," he said, "and Dr. Grayson has made it quite clear that I am to move as little as possible in case it affects my head and I become a lunatic!"

It seemed strange that he should prefer Peter's small Bed-Room to the very grand State Room in which Hermia knew he would be sleeping in her Uncle's home.

He lay looking at Peter's trophies, many of which were hung on the wall, and appeared to find everything to his liking.

In fact he did not complain about anything.

When he was well enough to talk he told the Earl and the Vicar exactly what had happened to him.

The Vicar related it to his wife and daughter that same evening.

"It seems even more incredible than we had imagined," he said, "except that it fits in with the despicable reputation enjoyed by de Ville."

"We are filled with curiosity, darling," Mrs. Brooke smiled.

"I will tell you everything," the Vicar replied, "but of course it took some time to extract it all from His Lordship because he had lapses of memory and we had to wait until he could think clearly again."

What Hermia and her mother learnt was that after the Earl had been summoned back to the Hall on what he now knew to be a pretext to inveigle him away, the Marquis had ridden on alone.

He rounded the end of Witch Wood to go in the direction where his host had told him the yearlings were to be found.

He was not hurrying, and it was therefore easy for three men to spring out at him from the bushes and, before he realised what was happening, to drag him off his horse.

Thinking they were footpads he fought violently, until they over-powered him and dragged him just inside the wood.

There was another man there who looked younger than the other three, but he did not see him very clearly before they forced him down onto the truck of a fallen tree.

"Two of the men," he related to the Vicar, "might have been foreigners or gypsies, the third seemed a superior type and better educated."

It was that man who produced a letter written on a piece of the Marquis's own writing-paper stolen from his house in London.

Because he had already been knocked about quite considerably the Marquis had a little difficulty in reading it, but he soon found it consisted of instructions to his trainer to withdraw his horse from the Gold Cup race at Royal Ascot.

Knowing his horse *Firefly* was favourite and having no doubt that with his usual luck he would win the Cup, he refused to sign the letter.

However, the men then began to punch him systematically until, knowing he had no chance against three of them, he agreed to do what they wanted, and wrote his signature at the bottom of the letter.

The minute he did so he felt something strike him

on the back of his head, there was a blinding pain and he knew no more.

"There was no doubt," the Vicar said as he related the story, "the whole plot was set up by Roxford de Ville for the simple reason that he owned a half-share in the horse that won the Gold Cup quite easily when the Marquis's did not run."

"I suppose he had it backed for a large sum," Hermia remarked.

"Of course!" the Vicar replied. "But in fact the plot was even more crooked than it appears, because the owners ran also another horse which they told everybody was better than the one that actually won!"

"Surely that is illegal?" Mrs. Brooke exclaimed.

"No, only unsportsmanlike," the Vicar replied. "The horse they tipped to all and sundry was unplaced, while the one that did win romped home at 16-1!"

"They must have made a fortune!" Hermia exclaimed.

"That is exactly what Roxford de Ville intended," the Vicar said, "but he was not so stupid as to give instructions that the Marquis should be murdered outright."

"Murdered!" Mrs. Brooke cried.

"Instead," the Vicar continued, "they carried him into what they had been told was the Witch's cottage and flung him down on the floor!"

He paused then he said slowly:

"They had already learnt that nobody from the village or the estate ever dared to visit old Mrs. Wombatt's cottage."

"I suppose anyone could tell them that," his wife exclaimed.

105

"It was murder by intent—a very difficult charge to prove," the Vicar said sternly, "for if Hermia had not been clever enough to think that was where the Marquis would be, he might easily have died during the night or would certainly have done so in two or three days time!"

Mrs. Brooke gave a cry of horror.

"It was a diabolical plot! What will the Marquis do about it?"

"John has been talking to the Chief Constable and they are considering if any charges can be brought against Roxford de Ville. Unfortunately it will be very difficult to prove that he was actually involved with the three men who have of course disappeared, having doubtless been well paid for their services."

"But if Mr. de Ville has failed . . . to murder the Marquis . . . this time," Hermia said, "he will surely . . . try again?"

"That is a possibility," her father agreed. "But in the meantime we must be concerned with getting the Marquis back on his feet. He is so healthy that I do not think it will take very long."

Having learnt from Hickson that the Marquis was not only better, but in the Valet's words: "Bored to his high teeth, Miss, if I may say so," Hermia went to see him.

It was late in the morning and her father and mother were both out, and Nanny had also gone shopping in the village.

She knocked tentatively on the Bed-Room door and when there was no answer went in.

The Marquis was in bed, propped up against several pillows.

Although the bandage had been removed from his

forehead there was still a pad at the back of his head.

He looked thinner and somewhat paler than she had last seen him.

But she thought when he glanced towards her that his eyes were still as penetrating as they had been before and made her feel shy.

"Come in, Hermia!" he said. "I was wondering when you would have time to visit me."

"Of course I had time, and I wanted to do so before," Hermia replied walking towards the bed, "but you had to be kept quiet and you were not supposed to talk to anybody."

"I am sick of being quiet!" the Marquis said petulantly. "And I want to talk to you!"

"I am here," Hermia smiled sitting down on a chair by the bedside, "and I thought perhaps you would like me to read to you."

"Later," the Marquis replied. "At the moment I should first thank you for saving my life."

She did not speak and after a minute he went on:

"Your father told me how in the middle of the night you went to what is called Witch's Wood and looked for me where nobody else would have dared to go. Why did you do that?"

"It . . . it is difficult to explain," Hermia replied, "but I was sure with a feeling which could not be . . . denied that it was where I would find . . . you."

"I am very grateful."

He spoke rather dryly, and she felt somehow that he was being cynical until he asked:

"Hickson tells me the whole village speaks of 'Witch Wood,' as they call it, with horror. Were you not frightened of going there alone at night?"

Hermia shook her head.

"I have loved the woods ever since I was a child, and I did not at all believe the stories that Mrs. Wombatt, who built the little cottage, really used to dance with the Devil."

"But you thought it was an appropriate place for me!" the Marquis remarked again in his mocking voice.

"I did not think of your nickname at the time," Hermia replied, "and I was not frightened until just before I opened the door!"

"Then what did you do?"

Because she thought the conversation sounded so serious and almost as if he was interrogating her she replied lightly:

"If I had thought of it, which actually I did not, I would have repeated the Cornish Litany which Mama taught me when I was a little girl."

She saw that the Marquis was listening and she therefore recited:

"'From Witches, Warlocks and Wurricoes,
From Ghoulies, Ghosties and Long-leggity
*   Beasties,*
From all Things that go bump in the night—
Good Lord deliver us!'"

When she finished the Marquis laughed.

"I can see that would be very effective, but as you did not say it, I presume you prayed that you would be safe and not shocked by what you found?"

"What really happened," Hermia said, "was that when I finally managed to remove the bar across the door, I put out my hand to open it and suddenly I felt frightened of what I would find inside."

She gave a little shudder as she remembered what she had felt.

"It was a nasty feeling, but then I heard an owl hoot in the trees and I knew there was no reason to be afraid for the animals in the wood would not be there if there was anything evil about."

She was silent for a second before she added:

"Also the fairies and elves have always protected me ever since I was a little girl."

She spoke naturally without thinking to whom she was speaking, then because she thought he would think her foolish she felt herself blush and said quickly:

"I found you and now you are safe."

"I can hardly believe what your father tells me, that you supported me all the way through the wood to the wall which borders the road!"

"You were very heavy," Hermia replied, "and if I have a crooked shoulder for the rest of my life, it will be all your fault!"

Again she was trying to speak lightly but the Marquis unexpectedly put out his hand towards her, laying it palm upwards on the white cover on the bed.

"Give me your hand, Hermia," he ordered.

Obediently she did so.

As his fingers closed over hers he said:

"Words are very inadequate with which to thank anybody for saving one's life and I am wondering how best I can express what I feel."

Because there was a deep note in his voice which Hermia had not heard before she felt a strange feeling she did not understand and her eye-lashes flickered as she said:

"Please . . . it would only make me very embarrassed, and really it is Mama you should thank for using her herbs and honey on you so cleverly that in . . . a day or two you will be as good as new."

Once again, because the Marquis was making her feel so shy, she was trying not to sound serious.

His hand tightened on hers, then he released her.

"Now," he said in a different tone, "tell me what happened when they first realised I was missing."

Because she thought it would amuse him, Hermia described what a flap there was at the Hall, her Uncle's agitation and how Marilyn had retired to bed.

"When Papa came home at eleven o'clock that night," she said, "Uncle John was planning a Military Operation to search for you, and I think, if the truth were known, rather fancying himself as a strategist!"

"But Marilyn retired to bed," the Marquis observed slowly.

"She was very upset," Hermia said quickly, "and I know she hopes you will go back to the Hall as soon as you are well enough to be moved."

"I am sure she does!" the Marquis remarked.

There was a little silence as Hermia wondered what to say next. Then he asked:

"How fond are you of your cousin?"

"I had a lovely time with her when we were young," Hermia answered. "We shared the same Governess, the same teachers, and of course it was marvellous for me to be able to . . . ride Uncle John's horses and use the . . . Library at the Hall."

She had no idea how wistful her eyes looked as she remembered what those two activities had meant to her.

"Then what happened?"

It flashed through Hermia's mind that he was perceptive enough to guess that she had been exiled as soon as Marilyn was grown up.

Because she thought even to talk of it would be humiliating she said quickly:

"I am sure you are talking too much. Let me read to you. It may be upsetting for you to hear what happened last week, but I have kept Wednesday's newspapers in case you wanted to hear about the Gold Cup."

"I am more interested at the moment in what has been happening here," the Marquis replied, "and I am trying to understand why your father and mother are so poor and have to skimp and save every penny when your Uncle is so rich."

Hermia stared at him. Then she said:

"You have been listening to Hickson who has been talking to Nanny! You must not believe everything he tells you."

"I use my eyes," the Marquis said, "and one thing is quite obvious: your Cousin Marilyn does not share her gowns with you!"

His words made Hermia immediately conscious that the gown she was wearing was very much the same as the one in which he had first seen her.

It was three years old and in consequence too tight, too short, and the colour had been almost washed out of it.

Because she thought it was not only tactless but impertinent of him to speak in such a way, her chin went up and she said:

"You may criticise, My Lord, but I promise you I would not change anything in my home for all the comforts at the Hall which are entirely material!"

"Is what you are seeking more important than the

luxuries of this world?" the Marquis asked.

Hermia felt she might have guessed he would not let such a statement pass and she replied:

"You will laugh, and because you are so rich you will not understand, when I say completely truthfully that money cannot buy happiness!"

There was silence as the Marquis stared at her and she felt once again that he was looking deep into her heart.

"Yet I suppose that being a woman," he said, "you would like pretty gowns, Balls at which to wear them, and of course a number of charming young men to pay you compliments."

Hermia laughed, and it seemed to echo round the small room.

"You are talking like Mama," she said, "who said she was wishing I could have magical gowns, magical Balls, and of course magical horses to ride."

She paused and there was a dimple in both her cheeks as she said:

"And actually that is exactly what I do have!"

Only for a second did the Marquis looked puzzled. Then he said:

"You mean in your imagination!"

Hermia thought it was quite clever of him to know that was what she meant, and she gave another little laugh before she replied:

"None of the magical things I have can be spoilt or taken away from me, and they never, never disappoint me. Also, My Lord, I should add they are very much cheaper!"

The Marquis smiled and now it was more than a twist of his lips.

"If I stay here very much longer," he said, "I have a feeling I shall be caught up in these magical spells and find it impossible ever to escape."

"You can always run away," Hermia said provocatively.

She paused before she went on more seriously:

"Perhaps a magical spell is what we must somehow give you before you leave, so that you will be safe . . . in case the wicked men who . . . attacked you once should do so . . . again."

She bent a little towards him as she added:

"Please . . . please, be very careful! The next time they might be more successful . . . in their . . . attempt to . . . destroy you!"

"If I were destroyed, I doubt if anybody would mourn me particularly," the Marquis said, "or miss me if I were no longer there."

Hermia sat upright.

"That is a ridiculous thing to say!" she said sharply. "Of course a great number of people would mourn you because they admire you for your sportsmanship, and even if they are envious, it makes them strive to better themselves."

She felt from the Marquis's expression that he did not believe what she was saying and after a minute she continued:

"I can tell you who would really miss you."

"Who?" the Marquis asked in an uncompromising voice.

Hermia had not the slightest idea that he was expecting her to say, as any other woman he had ever known would have said, that she would miss him.

"Your horses!" Hermia replied. "Nobody rides as

well as you do, could fail to love animals, and perhaps it is because your horses know you love them that they win so many races."

The Marquis did not speak and she went on reflectively:

"That was why I was quite certain the horse you were riding when you were attacked would not have thrown you!"

"It is certainly something I had never thought of before," the Marquis said quietly.

"Well, think about it," Hermia insisted, "and be careful if for nobody else's sake than for the horses who are waiting in your stables and longing for you to visit them again."

The Marquis was just about to reply when the door of the Bed-Room opened and the Earl came in.

He seemed very large and overpowering in the small room, and as Hermia hastily rose to her feet he looked at her, she thought, somewhat critically.

"Good morning, Uncle John!" she said, and kissed him on the cheek.

"Good morning, Hermia!" the Earl replied. "And how is your patient today?"

"As you can see he is very much better," Hermia said, "and Mama is very pleased with him."

"Good!" the Earl exclaimed. "That means with the Doctor's permission we can take him back to the Hall."

Hermia wanted to expostulate but quickly bit back the words.

Instead she said:

"I expect you would like to talk to His Lordship alone, and Dr. Grayson has insisted that he should not have more than one visitor at a time."

She went towards the door. When she reached it she turned to ask:

"Is there anything I can bring you, Uncle John? A cup of coffee, or perhaps a glass of port?"

As she mentioned the port she suddenly felt afraid her Uncle would be aware that it was his own port she was offering him.

Only last night when Hickson was serving their dinner in the Dining-Room as he poured some excellent Claret into the Vicar's glass he had said:

"I thought, Sir, you'd like a glass of port tonight, and I've filled the decanter."

"That sounds an excellent idea, Hickson!" the Vicar replied.

Then as he saw the expression on his wife's face he added:

"But I hope you had His Lordship's permission to bring the wines from the Hall."

"I'm sure 'Is Lordship would want my Master to have what he's used to, an' what 'e'd be drinking if he was there," Hickson answered. "But 'e doesn't like drinkin' alone and tells me while he were having his meal, I was to serve it to you, Sir."

Hickson spoke somewhat aggressively and Hermia suspected that in fact the Marquis had said nothing of the kind.

He had probably assumed that the Vicar would have wine with his meals just as he did.

He would have no idea that as far as the Vicarage was concerned wine was a treat they could only afford on special occasions, such as Christmas, birthdays, or when they entertained, which was practically never.

However the Earl replied:

"I want nothing, thank you, Hermia."

She shut the door and ran downstairs hoping fervently that her Uncle would not say anything to upset her father.

She knew however that her father did enjoy such luxuries.

Because she was thinking of him, almost as if she had conjured him up he came through the front door, shaking his hat because it had been raining.

"I see John is here!" he remarked.

Hermia was aware that the Earl's smart Phaeton, drawn by two well-bred horses with two men on the box, was waiting on the drive outside.

"Yes, he is talking to the Marquis, Papa, and has only been here a short while. So I should wait a minute or two before you join them, because Dr. Grayson said His Lordship was still to be kept as quiet as possible."

"I shall miss him when he goes," the Vicar remarked, walking into the Sitting-Room. "When I was talking to him yesterday, I realised he is a very intelligent man."

"I thought so too," Hermia replied.

It came into her mind that as the Marquis was intelligent he would find Marilyn if he married her, a bore.

She never read a book, was not interested in the political situation nor in anything that did not concern her Social Life.

Then Hermia told herself she was being unkind, and that Marilyn would make the Marquis a most agreeable wife, and would certainly look very pretty and graceful at the head of his table.

"I am sure they are well suited to each other," she tried to convince herself, but knew it was not the truth.

"Where is your mother?" the Vicar asked.

It was a very familiar question to Hermia because her father and mother missed each other if they were apart for even an hour or so during the day.

It was therefore the first thing each of them asked as soon as they returned home.

"Amongst other people, she has gone to see Mrs. Burles," Hermia answered. "She has been very bad the last few days because she is worrying over Ben."

"He is always a worry," the Vicar remarked, "but that is nothing unusual."

Hermia was aware that Mrs. Burles was terrified in her muddled mind that Ben would be in trouble because he had helped the men who had assaulted the Marquis.

She had said nothing to her father, and now changing the subject, she asked:

"Who have you seen today, Papa?"

"As usual the men, who are getting more and more desperate because they cannot find work," the Vicar replied. "I shall have to speak again to John, but God knows if he will listen to me!"

As he spoke he heard the Earl coming heavily down the stairs.

The Vicar walked from the Sitting-Room out into the hall to say:

"Nice to see you, John! As you see our patient is perking up and looking like his old self again."

"He certainly seems to be full of new ideas," the Earl remarked.

He did not go out through the open front-door as Hermia would have expected, but walked into the Sitting-Room and the Vicar followed him.

The Earl stood with his back to the fireplace and

117

there was a frown between his eyes before he said:

"Deverille and I were discussing the unemployment problem before I left him to be half-murdered at the instigation of his cousin."

"The unemployment problem?" the Vicar repeated in surprise.

"He was speaking about it again just now," the Earl went on, "and he is convinced that I should build a new Timber-Yard, because there is a great demand for wood now that the war is over."

Hermia listening, held her breath.

She could hardly believe she was actually hearing what her Uncle was saying.

"I find it difficult," the Earl continued, "not to follow up his suggestion. But as I have no time, and as this is something which will employ a lot of those layabouts with whom you are so concerned, Stanton, I am going to leave it to you!"

"Leave it to me?" the Vicar ejaculated.

Hermia knew that her father was as stunned as she was by what the Earl had just said.

"That is what I said," the Earl answered, "and you had better get on with it. Employ whom you like and as many as you like, but I shall expect the place to show a profit, or at least to break even within two or three years. Then we shall decide whether it is worth keeping it going."

The Vicar gave a deep sigh before he said:

"I can only thank you, John, from the bottom of my heart."

"Well, do not trouble me with the details," the Earl answered, "and make all the financial arrangements with my accountant. I will tell him to come down from London to see you."

With that, and as if he resented his own generosity, the Earl walked from the Sitting-Room, while his brother finding it hard to believe he was not dreaming, followed him.

Hermia clasped her hands together and knew that this was the Marquis's way of showing his gratitude.

Then, feeling she must tell him what it meant and how amazing it was, she ran from the room up the stairs to his Bed-Room.

She went in, shut the door behind her and stood for a moment just looking at him lying in the bed.

He did not appear for the moment to be either cynical or bored, and this in a way made her feel shy.

Nor for that matter did he seem like the stranger who looking like the Devil had dared to kiss her and whom she had hated!

As she did not speak, the Marquis turned his head, and she ran forward to kneel down beside the bed.

"How can you have done...anything so marvellous as to...persuade Uncle John to open a Timber-Yard?" she gasped. "It was wonderful...wonderful of you! And it will make Papa so...very happy!"

"And you," the Marquis questioned. "I see it has made you happy too."

"Of course it has, and I know Mama will go down on her knees and thank God, as I am...thanking you."

There were tears in her eyes as she looked at him and after a moment the Marquis said in his usual mocking manner:

"As you are so effusive over a Timber-Yard, I wonder what you would say if I offered you a diamond necklace?"

Because his remark was so unexpected Hermia sat back on her heels and laughed.

"At the moment I would rather have a Timber-Yard for Papa than anything in the world! Although I cannot wear it round my neck, I feel very, very proud that...perhaps what I...said to you made you...persuade Uncle John to do something for the men who...cannot find work."

The Marquis looked at Hermia, but he did not speak.

Then the door opened and Mrs. Brooke came into the room.

She was looking very pretty with her hair, which was nearly the same colour as her daughter's, a little untidy because she must have taken off her bonnet as she came upstairs.

She was holding it in her hand and now her cheeks were flushed and her eyes were shining as she said:

"I expect Hermia has already thanked you, as I am going to do."

"I think your husband should do that," the Marquis replied. "But please sit down, Mrs. Brooke, I want to talk to you."

Hermia rose to her feet as if she felt she should go away, but the Marquis said:

"You must stay, Hermia, because this concerns you."

He sounded serious and Hermia looked at him apprehensively wondering what he might be going to say.

A little nervously, in case he revealed something that her mother did not already know, she sat down on a chair.

Pushing himself up higher against his pillows the Marquis said:

"I have been thinking since I have been lying here what present I could give you as a family for all your kindness."

"We want nothing," Mrs. Brooke said quickly.

"That is what I might have expected you to say," the Marquis replied, "but I have a fixed rule in my life that I always pay my debts."

He paused, then added sourly:

"Unlike some people!"

Hermia thought he was referring to Roxford de Ville.

"I am only so glad that we have been able to do anything to help you," Mrs. Brooke said.

"I still, as it happens, value my life very highly," the Marquis answered, "and as Hermia is responsible for my being alive I would of course in normal circumstances have sent her a very expensive piece of jewellery to express my gratitude."

Mrs. Brooke would have spoken but he went on quickly:

"Instead I have another idea which I hope will meet with your approval, and as it happens, I know it will mean that one of your wishes will come true."

Hermia who was watching him as he spoke felt it hard to breathe as he continued:

"I have decided that what I will give Hermia is a few weeks in London until the Season ends."

Mrs. Brooke gave a little gasp and stared at the Marquis incredulously as he continued:

"I have a sister, Lady Langdon, who is a widow and who has been alone and unhappy since her husband was killed at the Battle of Waterloo. I know it would give her great pleasure to chaperon Hermia and introduce her to the Social World."

He gave a twisted smile before he added:

"She also, I believe, has very good taste in gowns, and would be delighted to find herself in the role of Hermia's Fairy Godmother!"

"It is . . . impossible!" Mrs. Brooke gasped. "Something we could not accept!"

"Nothing is impossible," the Marquis contradicted, "except that you should refuse to let your daughter have what is best for her. And this is an opportunity that should not be missed."

Because this was undoubtedly true, Mrs. Brooke could not reply and the Marquis went on:

"I will give a small Ball for Hermia at my house in London and my sister will make sure that she is invited to all those which take place before the Season ends. So there is only one thing we must do now."

"And what is that?" Mrs. Brooke asked and her voice seemed to come from very far away.

"We must get Hermia to London by the beginning of the week," the Marquis said. "There is not much of the Season left because the Regent will soon be leaving for Brighton, and after that a great number of people will shut up their houses and go to the country."

Again he smiled as he added:

"Therefore it is now up to your magic to get me on my feet, Mrs. Brooke, and then the Fairy Story, as far as Hermia is concerned, can start immediately!"

"I do not . . . believe what I am . . . hearing!" Mrs. Brooke said in a strange voice, and Hermia was aware that there were tears running down her mother's cheeks.

Only when Hermia went to bed that night, after she had talked over what the Marquis had planned with her father and mother until there seemed nothing left to say on the subject, did she go to her Bed-Room window and look out at the moon and the stars.

She had thought ever since the Marquis had told them his plan that she was living in a dream, and it was impossible to believe she was hearing that her prayers were about to come true.

And yet, just as if he had in fact waved a magic wand, the curtain was rising on a future so sparkling and so glorious that she felt as if she was being carried across the sky on a shooting-star.

The only thing that frightened her was what Marilyn would say, and whether when they heard what was happening her Uncle and Aunt would be angry.

Then she thought of the Timber-Yard which had pleased her father so much, and knew that the Earl had accepted to the Marquis's suggestion simply because he believed it came from the man he anticipated would be his son-in-law.

As she thought of it, it was as if a cold hand swept away the shining gossamer veil from her eyes and the stars were no longer shining so brightly.

Perhaps before he left the Marquis would propose to Marilyn, in which case it would not upset them that he was arranging for his sister to chaperone her.

"He is grateful . . . of course he is grateful to me," Hermia told herself, "and, as he says, he wishes to pay his debts."

She was working everything out in her mind in a

123

practical manner, but somehow that spoilt the rapture she felt.

Although it was something she seldom did, she pulled the curtain to and shut out the glory of the night, and got into bed in the dark.

As she lay sleepless she found herself wondering what the Marquis would say to Marilyn when he asked her to marry him, and what she would feel when he kissed her.

At the thought of it she could feel his lips hard, demanding and insistent on her own mouth.

She knew although he would never kiss her again, she would never forget he was the first man who had ever done so.

chapter six

HERMIA followed Lady Langdon into the large marble hall, and asked a footman:

"Is His Lordship back yet?"

"His Lordship came back a few minutes ago, Miss, and he's in the Study."

Hermia waited until Lady Langdon had set one foot on the stairs before she said:

"I wanted to speak to your brother, if you do not want me."

"No, we have finished all we had to do this morning, so go and talk to Favian," Lady Langdon replied with a smile, and walked up the exquisitely carved staircase which led to the State Rooms on the First Floor.

The Marquis's house was different from what Hermia had expected.

It was one of the largest mansions in Piccadilly, and even more magnificent and awe-inspiring than its owner.

On the Ground Floor there was the Dining-Room, the Library, the Breakfast and Writing Rooms, and the Study where the Marquis sat when he was alone.

All the Reception Rooms were on the First Floor, and the top of the double staircase seemed to have been designed for a hostess glittering in diamonds to receive her guests.

There were two Drawing Rooms adjoining each other which could be converted into a Ball-Room, large enough to hold at least two hundred guests, and beyond that were a Card-Room, a Music-Room, and to Hermia's delight a Picture Gallery.

It was all so well designed and decorated with exquisite taste that it seemed incredible that accustomed to living in such style the Marquis had seemed content with the small and shabby Vicarage.

The disadvantage of living in such a grand house was, as Lady Langdon pointed out, that all the bedrooms were on the Second Floor, and it was a long climb up and down unless one flew on wings—which Hermia felt she did.

Every day since she had arrived in London she had woken expecting to find herself in her small bedroom at home, and could hardly believe that what was happening to her was not just one of her fantasies that was more vivid than usual.

When the Marquis's carriage drawn by four horses had arrived at the Vicarage to take her to London she found he had also sent his elderly and very respectable Housekeeper to look after her during the journey.

At the last moment she had clung to her mother and said:

"I do wish you were coming with me, Mama. It

would be so much more fun if you were chaperoning me instead of the Marquis's sister."

"I would enjoy it, too," her mother answered, "but you know I could not leave Papa, and I am very, very happy that you are having a Season in London which I always imagined would be impossible."

To Hermia it had seemed impossible too! Moreover she was frightened that it would be overwhelming and that she would feel insignificant and make many mistakes in the world of which she knew nothing.

The welcome she received from Lady Langdon however warmed her heart.

"This is very exciting!" she exclaimed, as soon as she and Hermia were alone. "I have been so depressed and so lonely this last year that I could hardly believe it was true when I received an urgent note from my brother telling me what he had planned."

She had not waited for Hermia to reply, but continued:

"The first thing we have to do is to buy you a whole wardrobe of glorious gowns in which I know you will be the Belle of every Ball."

Because she was speaking sincerely and there was no doubt that she was genuinely delighted at the idea, she swept away all Hermia's nervousness and apprehensions.

The next morning they started very early to visit the shops in Bond Street.

Because it was near the end of the Season and the dressmakers were not so busy as they had been, Lady Langdon easily persuaded them to create gowns for Hermia in record time.

One of the dressmakers actually switched the dresses they had made for a bride so that Hermia could have

127

them at once, and they could repeat the models in time for the wedding.

By the time they had bought gowns, bonnets, shoes, gloves, shawls, pelisses, and reticules, Hermia felt as if her head was spinning.

She could no longer count what had been acquired and was actually, although it seemed ridiculous, feeling tired.

She found the fittings the following day more exhausting than riding, or indeed dancing.

Yet at her first Ball she knew she was the success her mother had wanted and she had many more partners than there were dances.

In the last five days she had been to three Balls, two Receptions, and there had been luncheon-parties either given by Lady Langdon or to which they had been invited as guests.

There had also been two dinner-parties given by other hostesses and Hermia felt she had lived through a lifetime of experience, and yet none of it seemed completely real.

Now as she walked down the passage decorated by some very fine pictures and exceptionally beautiful furniture, she thought that since she had arrived in London she had never had a conversation alone with the Marquis.

When they dined at home he sat as host at the top of the table, which invariably meant that he had two extremely attractive, sophisticated distinguished married women on either side of him.

When he accompanied his sister and Hermia to a Ball, he either retired almost immediately into the Card-Room or else, as had happened last night, he left early.

As Lady Langdon and Hermia drove home alone, she had asked curiously:

"Where do you think His Lordship has gone?"

Lady Langdon had given a little laugh.

"That is the sort of question you must not ask, dear Child," she replied. "As you can imagine, my brother has a great many lovely women praying and hoping that he will spend a little time with them."

Then as if she thought she had been indiscreet she said quickly:

"Unfortunately Favian soon becomes bored, and he is always looking for somebody new to amuse and entertain him."

She spoke lightly, but Hermia thought it was what she might have expected.

Yet if the Marquis was not particularly amused at this moment it was a good thing as far as Marilyn was concerned.

Marilyn had called to see the Marquis the day before he left the Vicarage, and as soon as she came through the front door Hermia was aware how angry her cousin was.

She was looking very attractive in a sprigged muslin that was made in the very latest fashion, and her bonnet, trimmed with pink roses, had a tipped up brim edged with lace.

She greeted Hermia in a frozen manner that could not be misunderstood.

Hermia opened the door of the Sitting-Room where the Marquis, having dressed and come downstairs, was resting in a chair in the window.

Marilyn had swept past her with a disdainful air which told her cousin more clearly than words what she thought of the Vicarage. Also how much she commiserated with anybody, especially the Marquis, who had been forced to stay in such a shabby and uncomfortable place.

Hermia shut the door behind her, then ran upstairs to her own room.

She wondered if the Marquis would take this opportunity to ask Marilyn to marry him, or perhaps make it clear that when he was in better health he would return.

Marilyn was with him for quite a long time and Hermia did not see her go. But the next day after the Marquis had left, she was quite certain from the way he said goodbye to her parents that he intended to come back.

That undoubtedly meant he wished to marry Marilyn.

"A nicer, more generous Gentleman I've never known in all me born days!" Nanny said positively after the Marquis had gone.

Hermia knew that she had received a sum of money for her services which had left her gasping.

She had learnt too from Nanny that there was still a great deal of wine in the cellar which had come not from the Hall, but from the Marquis's house.

It had been brought to the Vicarage by his secretary when he arrived to take instructions about her visit to London.

"It was very kind of the Marquis to think of it," she said to Nanny.

"Very kind," Nanny agreed, "but there's no reason for you to go chattering about it to your father. Let him think it was left over from His Lordship's visit. Them as asks no questions are told no lies!"

In the days before she departed for London Hermia

guessed the Marquis had made some other arrangements too, for the food remained as excellent as it had been when he was staying with them.

She thought this was due to some intrigue on the part of Nanny and Hickson.

But because she realised how much better her father looked and that the worried lines had disappeared from her mother's face, she took Nanny's advice and said nothing.

Now as she neared the Study door there was an expression in her eyes that would have told anybody who knew her well that she was feeling nervous and apprehensive.

She opened the door and saw that the Marquis was sitting at his desk writing.

"May I...speak to you for a minute? Or are you...too busy?" she asked.

There was a little tremor in her voice that he did not miss. He put down his pen and rose to his feet saying:

"How are you, Hermia? I must congratulate you on the gown you are wearing."

"I wanted to...ask how you are," Hermia replied, "and make quite certain you are not doing too much."

"If you fuss over me in the same way that Hickson is doing, I think I shall pack my boxes and leave England!"

"You cannot expect us...not to worry...about you!" Hermia answered.

The Marquis walked across the room to stand with his back to the fireplace which because it was summer was filled with flowers.

Hermia stood looking at him until he said:

"I can see you are upset about something. Suppose

you sit down and tell me about it?"

Hermia sat as he told her to do on the edge of a chair, her hands clasped together. She did not look at the Marquis, but at the flowers behind him.

After a moment he said pointedly:

"I am waiting!"

"I . . . I do not know how to . . . put what I . . . want to say into . . . words," Hermia stammered.

There was a little pause before the Marquis said:

"In which case I imagine you are about to tell me that you are in love. Who is the happy man?"

He was drawling the words. At the same time, there was the dry, cynical note in his voice which she had not heard for sometime.

"No . . . no," she said quickly, "it is nothing like . . . that! It does not concern me . . . at least not in the way you are . . . suggesting."

"Then I must apologise. I thought perhaps you wished me to give you my permission, in your father's absence, to marry one of the young men who were making love to you so ardently last night."

Because he was mocking her, and because it hurt her in a way she could not understand, Hermia clasped her fingers even tighter and said in a voice he could hardly hear:

"P–please . . . you are making it . . . very difficult for me . . . to say what I want to . . . say."

"Again my apologies," the Marquis said. "I will listen without guessing what it is you want to tell me."

"I am sure you will think it . . . terrible of me . . ." Hermia faltered, "and therefore . . . I am . . . afraid."

"It is unlike you to be afraid, Hermia," the Marquis replied. "In fact, I have always thought you exceptionally brave."

132

He gave one of his twisted smiles before he added:

"After all, if Witches, Devils and 'Things that go bump in the night' do not scare you, I cannot believe you are afraid of me!"

"I . . . am afraid of what you will . . . think."

"Why should that be so terrible?" the Marquis enquired.

She did not answer him, and after a moment he said in a softer and quieter voice:

"I hoped you would be happy here, not worried and frightened as you are now."

"I am happy!" Hermia said. "It has been so marvellous, so glorious to be able to dance at the Balls with new and fascinating people and to have such beautiful gowns!"

"Then what is wrong?"

"Your . . . sister who has been . . . kindness itself . . . has just said to me that she wants to buy me two more Ball-gowns to wear at the end of next week."

As she finished speaking Hermia seemed to draw in her breath before she said:

"Please . . . please . . . do not think it . . . ungrateful of me . . . but could you . . . instead of spending any more money on gowns for me give . . . Peter some new c–clothes?"

She did not dare to look at the Marquis in case he was scowling.

Instead she said pleadingly:

"It would not cost you any more, and I can manage . . . perfectly with the gowns I already have . . . but Peter would give . . . anything to be dressed like . . . you."

Still the Marquis did not reply, and now Hermia raised her eyes and he could see how desperately she was beseeching him to understand.

There was also the flicker of fear in their depths in case he should think her ungrateful and importunate.

"And you have been worrying about asking me this?" the Marquis enquired.

"Of course...I have," Hermia replied. "It...seems so greedy and ungrateful when you have done so much...but I do not wish Peter to feel...left out and as it is a terrible struggle for Papa to send him to Oxford...he can never afford any of the things his friends take for granted."

"I too was at Oxford," the Marquis remarked, "and I understand. You can leave Peter to me."

Hermia gave a little cry and jumped to her feet.

"You mean that...you really mean it?" she cried. "Oh...thank you...thank you!"

She paused before she asked in a very small voice:

"You...you do not think I am...imposing on you?"

"Shall I tell you," the Marquis replied, "that I am still deeply in your debt, and of course your mother's? The Doctor has told me this morning that there is nothing wrong with me, except that it would be a mistake to be hit in the same place again."

"Then you must be careful!" Hermia said quickly. "Promise me you will take care of yourself."

"First Hickson, and now you!" the Marquis remarked, but he was smiling.

"I keep thinking," Hermia said in a worried voice, "that you could be attacked perhaps in the Park when you are out riding, or when you come home late at night."

"I shall be all right," the Marquis said, "and all you have to do, Hermia, is to enjoy yourself and look

134

as beautiful as you do now."

Hermia looked at him wondering whether he meant it or was just flattering her.

As if he read her thoughts he said:

"Good Heavens! You must be aware that you have been an overnight sensation in the *Beau Monde* and my sister is delighted!"

"She has been very, very kind, but you will not forget to tell her I do not...require any more...gowns?"

"I doubt if she would listen to me," the Marquis replied, "and I have already told you that I will look after Peter."

"But...I do not mean it like that," Hermia cried. "He is not to be...an *extra* expense."

"I seem to remember your telling me," the Marquis said, "that money does not buy happiness, and material things are not important."

"Now you are quoting my words at me, in a different sense from what I meant them," Hermia said. "When you have done so much for me and my family I feel...ashamed of taking...anything more, and I know Papa and Mama would feel the same."

"I suppose what you are telling me is that you feel too proud," the Marquis said, "but I have my pride too, and I refuse to value my life at the cost of a few gowns, and a Ball which I might have given anyway, had I thought about it."

Hermia did not speak. She merely looked up at him and the Marquis said sharply:

"Stop trying to interfere! I enjoy making plans, and I cannot have them disrupted by rebellious young women who have other ideas than mine."

Hermia laughed.

"Now you are trying to frighten me again! But I refuse to be frightened! I was thinking last night that the Devil was originally an Archangel who fell from Heaven and now quite obviously he is climbing up Jacob's ladder to be there again."

"I am no angel," the Marquis retorted, "and I am quite content as I am. So stop trying to canonise me!"

"There is no need for me to do that," Hermia said. "I have a feeling that without my doing anything about it, there is already a halo firmly round your head, and wings sprouting from your shoulders."

"If there is," the Marquis said quickly, "it is some of the magic you are weaving around me until I am certain everything I drink contains a magic potion and there is witchcraft creeping into every corner of the house!"

"What a lovely idea!" Hermia exclaimed. "That is the right sort of magic, the magic which will bring you happiness and give you everything you wish for yourself!"

"I wonder!" the Marquis remarked reflectively.

Because there seemed to be nothing more to say, Hermia thanked him again, then ran up to her room to write a letter to Peter.

The Marquis, she thought, had been very kind, and now she felt as if she was enveloped in a golden light for the rest of the day.

Only when she came downstairs dressed in an exquisitely beautiful gown which she hoped he would admire, did she see Hickson coming from the Hall with the Marquis's evening-cape over his arm.

It seemed strange that he should be bringing it up the stairs now, and she stopped to say:

"Good evening, Hickson. Is His Lordship in the Drawing-Room?"

"No, Miss," Hickson replied. "I thought 'Is Lordship would have told you 'e's not dining here tonight."

"Not dining here?" Hermia asked. "But there is a party."

"Yes, I know, Miss, but His Lordship promised a long time ago to dine at Carlton House before 'Is Royal 'Ighness leaves for Brighton tomorrow."

"I understand," Hermia said, "but I hope he will come on later to the Ball I am attending."

"If 'e does, I think it would be a mistake for 'Is Lordship to stay up late and as he won't wear his cape he may catch a chill," Hickson spoke in exactly the same tone that Nanny might have used.

Hermia smiled.

"His Lordship is very much better," she said. "In fact he told me so today."

"All the same, 'e should take more care of 'imself," Hickson persisted.

Because the valet seemed as worried as she was, Hermia said:

"I am desperately afraid that the men who attacked him last time might try to do so again."

"That's right, Miss," Hickson agreed. "But 'Is Lordship never 'as a thought for 'imself, and when I tells 'im Mr. de Ville will murder 'im before 'e's finished, 'e just laughs."

Hermia gave a little exclamation.

"Do you really think that?"

"I does, Miss," Hickson said. "Mr. Roxford's tried it once, and he'll try again, you mark me words!"

"H–how can we . . . stop him?" Hermia stammered.

"You try speakin' to 'Is Lordship, Miss. 'e won't listen to me, says I'm an old 'fuss-pot', but it's no use fussing after a man's dead. You has to do something about it before that happens."

"Yes, of course," Hermia agreed, "but what can I do?"

Hickson gave a deep sigh.

"I don't know, Miss, an' that's a fact! I puts a loaded pistol beside the Master's bed at night, but he tells me anyone who attacks him in his bedroom would have to be a spider, or else fly through his window.

Hickson spoke in an aggrieved voice, but Hermia knew how fond he was of the Marquis. If he was apprehensive, so was she, feeling that the attack, having failed last time, would be repeated sooner or later.

"Does His Lordship carry a pistol with him when he is out riding?" she asked.

"I suggested it, but His Lordship says it spoils the shape of his coat!" Hickson replied. "However there's always one in the Phaeton, when His Lordship travels any long distance."

Hickson paused before he added:

"But the man who're attacking 'is Lordship don't want 'is money, but 'is life!"

Hermia gave a cry of horror, but there was no chance of saying any more because from where they were standing she could see the guests arriving for dinner.

Then as she walked into the Drawing-Room where Lady Langdon was waiting, Hermia felt that with the Marquis not there all the excitement had gone out of the evening.

She found this surprising, for she had been looking forward to it so much.

Then as she moved over the soft carpet she knew, although it seemed incredible, that unmistakably, irrefutably, she loved him.

*   *   *

Afterwards Hermia could never remember what she said at dinner or even who had sat on either side of her.

All she could think of was that she had fallen in love as she had always wished to do, but with a man who was as far out of reach as the moon.

She had hated him when he kissed her, she had thought him to be the villain in her fantasies, and she had been afraid of his sarcastic remarks and the way he looked at her.

Now she knew that only love could have guided her to the Witch's cottage, so that she could save his life.

Only love could have made it possible for her to support a man of the Marquis's size and weight back through the wood to safety.

She thought she had been very stupid not to realise why it had felt so exciting to have the Marquis, even though he was injured, at the Vicarage.

Then when he had persuaded the Earl to build a Timber-Yard, because it was what she had suggested to him, she should have known that what she felt for him was not only gratitude but love.

How could she have been so foolish as not to understand that beneath a disdainful facade he was warm-hearted, generous, compassionate and understanding?

It was not just magic that had changed everything and made the atmosphere in the Vicarage seem even happier and more exciting than it had ever been before, but her love for the man whose life she had saved.

'Of course I love him!' Hermia thought.

She knew that the men she had met and the compliments they had paid her had never seemed quite real. They were but cardboard figures stepping out from the pages of a book rather than flesh and blood.

The Marquis was real, so real that he had filled her thoughts, her mind, and her heart ever since she had known him.

However she tried to use her common sense and tell herself she could never mean anything to him and that he was going to marry Marilyn.

She had thought at first it was unlikely, but when he had persuaded her Uncle to open a Timber-Yard, she was quite certain it had been understood between them, even if it was not put into words, that the Marquis had got his way simply because the Earl wished to placate such an important son-in-law.

"I love him!" Hermia said to herself when they arrived at the Ball which was taking place in one of the most splendid and important houses in London.

Again there was all the glitter of jewels and decorations that she had found so entrancing and about which she had written pages and pages of description to her mother.

But tonight the chandeliers did not seem to shine and she found the decorations tawdry.

Although she had no shortage of partners, she had the greatest difficulty in showing any interest in what they said to her or listening to them.

She was wondering how soon it would be possible for her to go home, and if Lady Langdon would think it strange that she should not wish to dance until the early hours of the morning, when two men appeared in the doorway of the Ball-Room.

Hermia was dancing with Lord Wilchester, a young man who was paying her the most fulsome compliments.

"When may I see you alone?" he asked. "Can I call on you tomorrow?"

"I am not sure what we are doing," she replied vaguely.

"That is the same answer you gave me last night and the night before," he said. "I have something to say to you that I can only say when we are alone."

His fingers tightened on hers until his clasp was painful and Hermia realised that he intended to offer her marriage.

It flashed through her mind that as he was very rich and very important, it would be a marriage which would delight her father and mother and, of course, Lady Langdon.

But when she looked up into his eyes Hermia knew that if he pleaded with her for a hundred years she had no wish to be his wife.

"Lord Wilchester was paying a lot of attention to you," Lady Langdon had said last night as they drove home. "You have certainly made a conquest. I wish I could think that he might propose to you, but I am afraid that is aiming too high."

Hermia had not replied and Lady Langdon went on:

"Lord Wilchester is one of the most charming young men I have met for a long time. He has a large estate in Oxfordshire, besides owning Wilchester House in London which is quite exceptional."

She had sighed before she added:

"But it is expecting too much! Every ambitious mother in London has been trying to capture him for their daughters, and I think if he marries anybody it will be one of the Duke of Bedford's daughters."

Hermia had not thought about it again, but now she knew without Lord Wilchester saying any more what he intended.

'I should accept him to please Papa and Mama,' she thought.

She looked up to see the Prince Regent coming into the Ball-Room, and behind him the Marquis.

Because she was so glad to see him and because everything else faded away from her mind she forgot Lord Wilchester and what he was saying to her until as if his voice came from a long way away she heard him say:

"I asked you a question!"

"I . . . I am sorry," she said quickly. "I did not . . . hear what you said."

Again she was watching the Marquis talking to their hostess, and she saw as he did so that his eyes were searching the Ball-Room as if he was looking for her.

Then she told herself that if Lady Langdon thought Lord Wilchester was out of reach, even more so was the Marquis.

She did not miss the innuendos she had heard almost every evening at dinner, or at any luncheon party she attended.

"You are staying at Deverille House?" her partners always exclaimed. "Good gracious, you must be a very important person!"

"Why should you think that?" Hermia had asked, knowing the answer.

"Deverille is never seen with young women. In fact, it is always said in the Clubs that he would not know a young woman if he saw one!"

Then usually the man who had thus spoken would look embarrassed and say quickly:

"Perhaps I am being rude. Of course, as Lady Langdon is chaperoning you, that means you are a relative."

Hermia had not troubled to contradict that idea.

She did not miss either the disagreeable and jealous looks she received from the beautiful women who clustered round the Marquis when he introduced her to them.

"Miss Brooke is my guest," he would explain, and a look of curiosity would be replaced by one of incredulity or of unconcealed antagonism.

Hermia thought she could not imagine women could look so beautiful or so alluring and not hold every man irresistibly captivated by their charms.

There was no doubt they set out to entice the Marquis, and watching them Hermia thought for the first time that she could understand what the temptations of St. Anthony had been like.

Or to put it in a more familiar way, she thought that the lovely Sirens who surrounded the Marquis pictured the villager's imagination of the Witches who revelled with Satan in Witch Wood.

They fluttered their long, dark eye-lashes at the Marquis, pouted at him with reddened lips and the gowns they wore seemed almost indecently *décolleté*.

It told Hermia quite clearly that despite the beautiful gowns she had been given, she was no more than the stupid, inconsequential village girl whom the Marquis had once mistaken for a milk-maid.

"That is how he thinks of me," she thought.

Then she felt as if she went down into a little Hell of her own, where there was no requited love, only the frustrations of yearning and wanting what was out of reach and unobtainable.

Although the Marquis smiled in her direction at the Ball he made no move to speak to her and when the Prince Regent left he left with him.

Later Lady Langdon and Hermia drove home alone, and as the two horses drew the comfortable carriage swiftly down Piccadilly Lady Langdon said:

"You looked very lovely tonight, and the Duchess said you were undoubtedly the prettiest girl in the room! I noticed too that Lord Wilchester was very attentive."

"He asked if he could call and see me tomorrow," Hermia said without thinking.

Lady Langdon gave a little exclamation.

"He asked to see you alone?"

"Yes, but I do not wish to be alone with him!"

"My dear Child, do not be so ridiculous! Can you not understand that he is going to propose to you? He would never ask to see you alone otherwise."

"I thought perhaps he was thinking of something like that," Hermia said in a low voice, "but...I do not wish...to...marry him."

"Not wish to marry Lord Wilchester?" Lady Langdon cried in amazement. "But my dearest Hermia, you must be off your head! Of course you must marry him! It would be the most marvellous, brilliant marriage to which you could aspire! In fact I will be honest and say that I had no idea you could capture the heart of the most elusive bachelor in the whole of the *Beau Monde!*"

She paused, then added almost as if it was a joke:

"With, of course, the exception of my brother, who has sworn he will never marry!"

"Why should he do that?" Hermia asked with a different note in her voice from what there had been before.

"Has no one told you that poor Favian was abominably treated by a girl to whom he lost his heart the year after he came down from Oxford?"

"What happened?"

"It was quite an ordinary story, but had consequences we never envisaged at the time."

"What were they?"

"Favian fell in love with the Duke of Dorset's daughter. She was lovely, quite lovely, but I always thought she was not quite what she appeared."

"I do not understand," Hermia murmured.

"Caroline was very beautiful, looked magnificent on a horse, which of course pleased Favian, and appeared to be as much in love with him as he was with her."

Lady Langdon gave a little sigh.

"The whole family was delighted because Favian had just come into the title and being so rich and so attractive was being pursued by every woman he met."

She paused before she went on:

"We all thought if he settled down and spent more time in the country than in London it would be excellent for him, and perhaps prevent him from going into the Army, as he wished to do."

"Did they become engaged?" Hermia asked.

"Not officially. The families of both sides knew it was an understanding, and in fact the announcement was due to go into the *Gazette* when Favian discovered that Caroline was behaving in an outrageous manner with the man with whom she was really in love!"

Hermia made a murmured exclamation, and Lady Langdon continued:

"I could hardly believe that any well-bred girl would stoop to having a love affair with a man of a different class all together, and disgrace herself by meeting him surreptitiously in the ground of her father's estate."

"Who was he?"

"He was her father's horse-trainer and of course Caroline had often been escorted by him when she went riding."

Hermia could see what had happened and Lady Langdon said in a tone of the most utter contempt:

"It was disgraceful, absolutely disgraceful that any Lady should behave in such a manner! I learnt, although Favian could never talk about it, that he had received an anonymous letter from somebody who was jealous of him, and he surprised Caroline and the man she loved in very unfortunate circumstances."

"It must have hurt him very much," Hermia murmured.

"It made him extremely cynical, and he immediately joined the Army and fought in the Peninsula and France until Wellington was victorious at Waterloo."

"I had no idea he was a soldier."

"The Duke of Wellington told me he was an excellent officer in every way, but although he came back to enjoy the good things of life that were waiting for him, I have always felt he was somewhat contemptuous of them."

It was what Hermia had thought herself. Then she said, because she could not help asking the question:

"Has the Marquis never fallen in love with anybody else?"

"There have been many women in his life," Lady Langdon replied. "In fact, they never leave him alone! We have been hoping and praying that he will marry, if only to prevent that ghastly cousin of ours, Roxford de Ville, from borrowing money as Favian's heir presumptive."

There was a pause before Lady Langdon said:

"I rather hoped he might marry that pretty cousin of yours. In fact, when he told me he was going to stay with her father I hoped it was she who attracted him rather than your Uncle's horses, of which Favian has quite enough already!"

There was no need for Hermia to reply, because at that moment the horses drew up outside the Marquis's house.

"We are home," Lady Langdon announced, "and I must admit I am ready for bed."

They walked up the staircase together and climbed the next flight to the Second Floor.

The rooms there were equally impressive with high ceilings and, as was to be expected, exquisite decoration.

When she reached her own bedroom Hermia felt that for all the pleasure it gave her it might as well have been an attic with nothing in it but an iron bedstead.

All she could think of was the Marquis being disillusioned and disgusted by the girl with whom he had fallen in love and in consequence swearing that he would never marry anybody.

When her maid who had waited up to undo her gown had left her, Hermia went to the window to pull back the curtains.

Once again, as she had done before she looked at the new moon that was just rising up in the sky and thought that just as it was out of reach, so was the Marquis.

'I may love him, but he will never love me!' she thought.

Then she thought that Lord Wilchester was coming tomorrow to propose to her and she felt herself shudder.

"I cannot marry him, I cannot!" she told herself passionately.

Then she saw herself at the Vicarage spending the rest of her life carrying soothing syrups and salves to Mrs. Burles and a dozen other women like her.

Or waiting for her mother or her father to come home in the evening, knowing that while they both loved her and she meant a great deal to them, they would rather be alone with each other.

'I should marry him,' she thought.

Then she looked at the sky through the uncurtained window and thought that she could see the Marquis's face amongst the stars.

"Out of reach!"

She could almost hear him saying the words mockingly in that dry voice of his that made her feel shy.

"Out of reach! Out of reach!"

chapter seven

H<small>ERMIA</small> found it impossible to sleep.

She twisted and turned, and all she could think of was the Marquis and that if she married somebody else or returned to the Vicarage she would never see him again.

She was also afraid for him, and although he might laugh at Hickson's concern she kept thinking of how every hour of every day he was in danger from his cousin.

Because she had been thinking about him the previous night she had said to an elderly man who was at the Ball she was attending:

"Is Roxford de Ville here by any chance?"

He looked at her in surprise before he answered:

"I cannot imagine our hostess would contemplate having such a disreputable character as one of her guests!"

Hermia did not speak and after a moment he laughed and said:

"Anyway, this is not the sort of company in which de Ville feels at home."

She looked at him for explanation and he explained:

"He spends his entire life in low Night Clubs, with the gypsies on Hampstead Heath, or I have heard recently with the trapeze artists who perform at Vauxhall Gardens."

"Why does he like those sort of people?" Hermia enquired.

Her companion went into a long explanation of how disreputable the Marquis's cousin was and how much he was disliked.

But Hermia was remembering that the Marquis had told her father that two of the men who had knocked him about were swarthy and might have been foreigners or gypsies.

She wondered if she should warn the Marquis that it would be a mistake to go anywhere near Hampstead Heath, but she doubted if he would listen to her.

She was sure he would merely laugh and say he could look after himself.

'If Roxford de Ville is determined to murder him, he will do so,' she thought.

The idea made her want to cry because she felt so helpless.

Throwing off the sheets because it was hot she climbed out of bed and went to the open window.

She told herself it was because she needed air, but actually she wanted to look at the moon and think about the Marquis.

She had to force herself to accept the fact that he was out of reach.

Then as she leaned out of the window she looked along the back-wall of the house towards the far end where she knew the Marquis was sleeping.

She had learnt that when he had inherited he had not altered the front of the house which faced onto Piccadilly and was very impressive.

The back was rather featureless, but he had added to it the wrought iron balconies which had just come into fashion.

Hermia had learnt that all the houses that were being built in Brighton, and there were a great many because the *Beau Monde* followed the Prince Regent there, had wrought iron balconies.

Those the Marquis had added were all of beautiful workmanship and the windows of the State Rooms on the First Floor now had large balconies with elaborate designs rising to about three feet around them.

Those on the Second Floor where she was sleeping were only half as big, but equally elaborate.

On the floor above there was only a token surround outside each window.

The effect from the garden was very impressive.

But as Hermia leaned out of the window she thought the Marquis had been very clever to improve his London house so outstandingly.

Then as she looked at his bedroom, which was on the same level as her own, she raised her eyes and thought that a chimney had fallen forward onto the balustrade of the roof.

She wondered vaguely if anybody was aware of it, and determined in the morning, to tell the servants to make investigations.

Then what had appeared to be a heap of stone moved, and she realised it was not a fallen chimney as she had thought, but a man leaning over from the roof to look down below him.

For a moment she thought he might be a workman, but it was a strange time of night for men to be working on the roof.

Then she saw in the moonlight there was not one man, but two.

'Something must have happened,' she thought.

Then as she stared, finding it hard to see clearly from the angle at which she was looking, she suddenly remembered what her partner had said last night.

"Trapeze artists at Vauxhall Gardens!"

She started and felt a streak of fear run through her as she knew that this constituted a danger for the Marquis.

She could hear Hickson saying to her that his master had said that no one could enter his bedroom unless they were a spider, or flew in through the window.

"That is what his cousin intends to do!" Hermia told herself in terror.

She took one last look and now she could see that one man was on the very edge of the balustrade and she thought that there were ropes around his shoulders.

It was obvious that the other man was beginning to let him down slowly towards the Marquis's bedroom window.

With a cry that was stifled in her throat, she turned and, pulling open her bedroom door, lifted up her nightgown and started to run down the passage which led to the other end of the house.

It was quite a long way, and as she ran she felt frantically that if she should be too late either Roxford de Ville, or whoever he had hired to kill the Marquis, would have performed the evil task before she was able to save him.

She thought the murderer was most likely to enter the bedroom and stab the Marquis because that would make no noise.

And yet she could not be sure. It would be quicker and perhaps easier, to shoot him from the balcony.

Then the criminal would immediately be hauled back up onto the roof before anybody would think of looking for him in such an unlikely place.

It all flashed through her mind as she ran with her heart thumping violently against her breast over the soft carpet, past Lady Langdon's room, past the empty spare rooms which came before the Marquis's Suite.

She knew where his bedroom was because Lady Langdon had taken her round the house and had shown her the Marquis's room saying:

"This is the Master Suite where my father, my grandfather and my great-grandfather all slept. It is the one place in the house that Favian has not changed, but left very much as it was, and I love it because it brings back so many memories of my childhood."

She remembered it was a large, very impressive room with one window looking onto the garden, and another on the side of the house from which there was a glimpse of Green Park.

What had impressed Hermia most was the huge four-poster bed curtained with crimson velvet, the back embellished with an enormous replica of the Marquis's coat-of-arms in colour.

It seemed almost regal and a most fitting back-ground for him, and now as she ran faster and even faster she thought it might be his death-bed.

She opened the door.

The room was in darkness except for the moonlight coming through one open window.

It was the window which looked onto the garden, and even as Hermia moved towards the bed to awaken the Marquis she saw the stars outside being obscured by a dark form which she knew was a man's legs coming onto the balcony.

Because she was so breathless it was almost impossible to speak.

"My . . . Lord!" she whispered and because she was so frightened she could not even hear herself.

Then as he did not answer she knew with a terror that seemed to strike into her body like the point of a dagger that the light from the window was now almost completely blocked out and she whispered again:

"My . . . Lord! My . . . Lord! Wake . . . up!"

She put out her hand as she spoke to shake him because he must be sleeping so heavily.

Instead of touching his shoulder, however, as she had intended to do, she found her hand was touching something hard and cold that was lying on a low table by the bedside.

Her fingers closed over it almost before her mind told her that it was the loaded pistol which Hickson had told her was always there.

As she took it up in her hand looking frantically towards the window, she realised the man outside had shaken off the ropes by which he had descended.

She saw something glint in his hand and knew it was a dagger.

It was all happening so swiftly that she hardly had time to think but only to be aware of the danger coming towards the Marquis whom she could not waken.

Lifting up the pistol she pointed it towards the intruder and just as he stepped forward to enter the room she pulled the trigger.

There was a resounding explosion that seemed almost to break her ear-drums. Then the man in the window gave a shrill cry, and Hermia shut her eyes.

Trembling she opened them and there was only the moonlight once again coming into the room.

It was then, with her ears still ringing from the explosion, that she looked towards the bed and saw a door on the other side of it was open and silhouetted against the golden light in the room behind him was the Marquis.

For a moment she could hardly believe that he was there and not asleep as she had expected him to be.

Then she threw the pistol down on the bed and ran towards him, to fling herself against him.

"He was going to . . . kill you," she cried. "He was . . . going to . . . kill you!"

The Marquis put his arms around her and as she felt the strength of them and knew he was safe, Hermia burst into tears.

She hid her face against his shoulder sobbing:

"He was . . . let down by a . . . rope from the . . . r– roof . . . I saw him and thought I would never get . . . here in time . . . and he would kill you . . . while you . . . slept."

Her words seemed to fall over each other and they were broken by sobs which made her whole body tremble beneath her thin nightgown.

"But you were in time," the Marquis said quietly, "and once again, Hermia, you have saved my life."

He held her close for a moment. Then he said:

"I must go to see what has happened, but do not

move until I tell you to do so."

He sat her down gently on the side of the bed and while she still cried he walked away from her to look out of the window.

He did not speak and she suddenly thought the whole thing had been a dream and there had been no man there, that she had just imagined it.

She was afraid the Marquis would think she was very foolish and hysterical to behave in such a manner.

Then she remembered that if it was real and she had killed a man the repercussions would be frightful.

She stopped crying, but the tears were still on her cheeks as the Marquis came from the window.

She saw that he was wearing a dark robe which reached the ground, making him somehow more impressive than usual.

She looked up at him beseechingly and now he could see her face clearly in the light which came from his Sitting-Room.

"It was very brave of you, Hermia," he said quietly. "My Cousin Roxford is dead. No one could fall from such a height and not break his neck."

"I . . . I have . . . killed him!" Hermia whispered.

"No," the Marquis answered. "You surprised him but your bullet went into the side of the window-frame and actually did not touch him."

She stared at the Marquis as if she could not believe what she had heard.

Because she could not speak he put his arm around her and drew her gently to the window.

She could see the rope which Roxford de Ville had shrugged from his shoulders before he was ready to enter the bedroom.

Then the Marquis pointed a little above her head, and Hermia could see quite clearly in the moonlight that the wooden lintel was splintered where the bullet she had fired had entered it.

Because she was so relieved that she had not actually killed anybody, even if it was a man with murder in his heart, she turned her face once again towards the Marquis's shoulder.

He knew she was thinking that now she would not have to stand trial or explain what had happened and his arms tightened around her as he said:

"I want you to understand that you must not be involved in any way."

He looked out of the window before he went on:

"They will find my cousin in the morning, and the ropes from the balcony outside the room. The story I shall tell is that he must have lost his balance coming down from the roof."

Hermia lifted her face to look up at him.

"Everybody will . . . know he intended to . . . kill you."

"Officially nobody must know that," the Marquis said sharply. "The Magistrates will be told that it amused him to climb over roofs and play pranks on people at night, and having had too much to drink he slipped and fell."

"They will . . . believe that?"

"I will make sure they do so."

"Now . . . you are safe . . . and nobody will . . . try to kill you?"

"I hope not," the Marquis answered, "but as I do not wish you to be questioned you are to go back to bed and forget what has happened. We will talk about it again in the morning."

"But ... will you be ... safe?" Hermia said almost beneath her breath.

"I shall be safe," the Marquis repeated, "because you have saved me."

He looked down at her. Then as she stared up at him in the moonlight his lips came down on hers.

For a moment she could hardly believe what was happening.

Then as the Marquis kissed her for the second time she knew this was very different from the kiss he had given her before.

Because she loved him her lips were very soft and warm as she felt his mouth take possession of hers and she knew that it was what she wanted more than anything else in the whole world.

It was what she had yearned for, prayed for, and now as he kissed her she felt as if she surrendered herself to him completely and gave him not only her heart, but her soul.

It was so perfect, so exactly as she had felt a kiss should be, and yet a million times more wonderful than she had ever imagined.

She at the same time, felt as if the moonlight moved through her body in a silver stream and the stars fell out of the sky to shine in her breast and join her lips with the Marquis's.

It was so perfect, so ecstatic, so unbelievably rapturous, that she felt if she died at this moment, she would be in Heaven and would never have to return to earth.

Then as she moved closer and still closer to the Marquis he raised his voice and said in a voice which seemed strangely unlike his:

"Go to bed! Forget what has happened and nobody must know that you have been here in my room tonight."

Because what she felt when he kissed her made Hermia speechless and in a daze she could not answer him.

She was only aware that he drew her across the room to open the door and very gently push her outside.

"Do as I have told you," he commanded.

Then almost before she could realise what was happening his door had shut behind her and she was alone in the corridor.

It was difficult to think, difficult to be aware of anything but the emotions pulsating through her and feeling that her lips were still held captive by the Marquis.

Somehow she walked back along the corridor finding her way now by the light of the candles guttering low in the silver sconces which she had not noticed when she had run to save the Marquis.

She reached her bedroom and only the open window and the moonlight coming through it told her that what she had seen when she had looked along the wall of the house, had been real.

Even though the Marquis had not been in his bed his cousin could have stabbed him in the other room when he was weaponless.

Quickly Hermia got into bed, then as she shut her eyes she could only think that the Marquis had kissed her and nothing else was of any importance.

*   *   *

Hermia was awoken as usual by the maid who looked after her.

She came in and set down by the bedside the hot chocolate she always brought Hermia before she rose.

As she did so she said as if she could not prevent herself from speaking about it:

"Oh, Miss, there's such a to-do downstairs! Everybody's in a turmoil!"

"What has happened?" Hermia asked and managed to speak quite naturally.

"It's His Lordship's cousin, Miss. He's been found dead in the garden after falling off the roof!"

"How terrible!" Hermia exclaimed. "But why was he on the roof?"

"Mr. Hickson says it's all them tricks them trapeze people 'as taught him. Them as performs in Vauxhall Gardens."

Hermia smiled a little as the maid chatted on, feeling sure that Hickson would be the only person who might guess what was the real truth, even though he would not know she was involved in it.

Lady Langdon insisted that after they had a late night neither of them had breakfast until late in the morning.

Now as Hermia waited for the maid to tell her her bath was ready, she said:

"Oh, I almost forgot to tell you, Miss—His Lordship says neither Her Ladyship nor you are to come downstairs before luncheon. Mr. de Ville's body is being taken away as soon as the Undertakers arrive. Until then he wants you to stay upstairs."

As she finished speaking she went to the door saying:

"I'll bring your breakfast, Miss, as soon as it's

ready, but I thinks as 'ow Her Ladyship's still asleep."

Hermia lay back amongst the pillows with a little sigh of relief.

In spite of what the Marquis had said, she had been afraid that Roxford de Ville might be injured and not dead, and would live to try to kill again.

Now the Marquis was safe, and it suddenly came into her mind that there would now be no pressure on him to marry, and he could continue to enjoy his freedom as he had before.

She thought Marilyn would be disappointed, but she knew that while the Marquis need not marry Marilyn, he would also not think of marrying her.

He had kissed her, but that was a kiss of gratitude, and she was quite certain that if he had loved her, he would have said so.

Instead he had sent her to bed and told her never to think or speak of what had happened again.

"I will never speak of it," Hermia said to herself, "but I will never . . . forget that he . . . kissed me . . . and how could I ever feel the same for . . . another man?"

Then with a little feeling of apprehension she remembered that Lord Wilchester was coming today to propose to her.

She thought in the circumstances it would be reasonable to say that no visitors should be admitted to the house.

Then a frightening thought struck her.

However disreputable he might be, Roxford de Ville was a member of the Marquis's family, and he and his sister would now be in mourning.

This meant that it would be impossible for Lady Langdon to take her to any more Balls or parties, at least until after the Funeral.

'I shall have to go home!' Hermia thought and felt her spirits drop.

It was as if the sun was eclipsed and there was only darkness outside.

She would say goodbye to the Marquis and go home, and that would be the end.

"I cannot bear it! How can I . . . leave him?" she asked, but knew she had no alternative.

When she came downstairs just before luncheon it was to find, as she had expected, that Lady Langdon had cancelled the luncheon party they were to have had, and she and Hermia ate alone.

There was no sign of the Marquis and as she and Lady Langdon sat in the big Dining-Room and for the first time since her arrival there was nobody else with them, Hermia felt as if she was already on her way back to the Vicarage.

Lady Langford could talk of nothing but the strange behaviour of Roxford de Ville which had made him climb over the roof at night.

It never seemed to strike her that he might have had a sinister motive for doing so.

"He has always been unpredictable," she chatted in her usual manner, "but who but Roxford would wish to associate with trapeze artists and the gypsies of whom most people are afraid?"

"It certainly seems strange," Hermia murmured.

"When I saw Favian this morning he said it was obvious Roxford had had too much to drink and was therefore unsteady on his feet, and considering the way he has behaved recently he might easily have died in far more disreputable circumstances! We can only be thankful that it was no worse than it was."

"Yes . . . of course," Hermia agreed.

"It has certainly upset our plans for today," Lady Langdon said. "But we must find out what Favian thinks we can do tonight. I have no intention of cancelling more parties than is absolutely necessary for propriety's sake. No one will mourn Roxford, least of all his relatives."

Lady Langdon rose to leave the Dining-Room as she spoke and when they reached the Hall she said to the Butler:

"When His Lordship returns tell him Miss Brooke and I will be in the Library."

"Very good, M'Lady," the Butler replied.

They went to the Library, and another time Hermia would have been happy to browse amongst the books and find a new one to read.

But she could only wonder what the Marquis would have to say when he returned and hoped he would not be long.

She desperately wanted to see him but at the same time she felt shy.

Then she told herself that while his kiss had taken her into the sky and she had touched the Divine, to him it had been just an expression of gratitude.

"I must not behave towards him," she told herself, "in any way which would make him feel embarrassed."

She went on reasoning it all out:

"If I cling to him, if I show that I love him, I will just be like all those other women who fawn on him and with whom he is quickly bored."

But she knew it was going to be very difficult.

Lady Langdon put down the magazine she had been reading.

"As I have nothing particular to do," she said, "and

because as we got to bed so late I am rather tired, I think I will go and lie down. Tell Favian when he comes that if he has anything important to tell me he can wake me up. If not, I will be down in time for tea."

"I will tell him," Hermia replied.

She opened the door for her hostess and Lady Langdon said:

"You have not forgotten that Lord Wilchester will be calling on you? I do not expect he will arrive before three o'clock, which is the correct time for such visits."

She walked away before Hermia could ask her to tell the servants she was not at home.

Quite suddenly she was frightened.

'I cannot see him,' she thought. 'If he asks me to marry him and I refuse it will be very embarrassing, and it would be much better to prevent him from speaking to me.'

She waited until she thought Lady Langdon would have reached her bedroom, then rang the bell.

The Butler answered it and she said to him:

"I am expecting Lord Wilchester to call at about three o'clock. If he does, will you tell him that in the circumstances I am not at home to any visitors?"

"Yes, I'll tell him, Miss," the Butler replied.

As he spoke through the open door behind him came the Marquis.

He was looking very elegant and Hermia thought more exquisitely dressed than usual.

But it might have been because just to look at him made her heart turn several somersaults in her breast, and she felt as if the room was suddenly lit by a thousand lights.

"What is this?" he asked. "Who are you refusing to see?"

It was somehow impossible for Hermia to answer him, and the Butler replied for her:

"Miss Brook understood Lord Wilchester was calling, M'Lord, but I'll inform His Lordship she's not receiving."

"Yes, do that," the Marquis agreed.

The Butler shut the door and the Marquis walked towards Hermia. She watched him, her eyes filling her face.

Then as he reached her he said:

"You are all right?"

"Y—yes . . . of course."

"But you have no wish to see Wilchester! Why?"

She felt his eyes looking at her in the penetrating manner which always made her feel shy, and she looked away from him.

Then as she realised the Marquis was waiting for an answer to his question she said:

"I . . . I thought it was . . . correct."

"Is that the only reason?"

As if he compelled her to reply she said:

"I . . . I did not . . . wish to . . . see him alone."

"Why not?"

It was difficult to find an answer. Then as she was silent after a moment the Marquis said:

"Last night when I returned after you had gone to bed, my sister left me a note to say that Wilchester had asked to see you alone today and she was sure he intended to propose marriage. Is that what you expect?"

"Y—yes."

The monosyllable seemed to be drawn through lips that trembled, but still Hermia dared not look at the Marquis.

"He is very important in the Social World and a man whom other men admire. I doubt if you will have a much better offer."

The way the Marquis spoke made Hermia feel as if every word was a blow that hurt her most unbearably.

She also realised he was drawling his words and speaking in the same, dry, cynical manner as he had done when they first met.

When she did not speak the Marquis said:

"Well? Are you going to accept him? I am interested to know."

"I– it is what your sister thinks I should do," Hermia answered, ". . . but it is . . . impossible."

"Why impossible?"

Hermia drew in her breath.

"Because . . . I do not . . . love him."

"And you think that is more important than all he can give you? Security, money, a position which most women would fight frantically to attain?"

Hermia clenched her fingers together until her knuckles dug into the palms of her hands.

"I know you will . . . think me . . . very foolish," she said, "but . . . I could not marry anybody . . . unless I . . . loved them."

"What do you know about love?" the Marquis asked. "When I was in the country I was sure it was something of which you were very ignorant. I am equally certain that I am the only man who has ever kissed you!"

His words made the colour flood into Hermia's cheeks and she wanted to run away before she could be questioned any further.

At the same time, she wanted to stay simply because she was with him.

"Now, strangely," the Marquis went on, "you know . . . you do not love one of the most charming young men in the whole of the *Beau Monde!* How can you be so sure?"

There was a very easy answer to that, Hermia thought, but it was something she could not say.

She could only feel herself tremble and hope the Marquis was not aware of it.

Then in a voice that she had never heard him use before he said:

"Last night, Hermia, when I kissed you I thought it was very different from the first time, even though to me that was an unexpected enchantment which I have found it impossible to forget."

Because she was so surprised Hermia looked up at him for the first time.

As her eyes met his it was impossible to look away and she felt as though he was looking deep down into her soul and knew how much she loved him.

"After last night," the Marquis went on, "I might have been mistaken, Hermia, but I was sure you loved somebody, even though you are afraid to admit it."

She could only stare at him, her lips slightly parted, her heart pounding in a manner that made it impossible to speak, or even to breathe.

The Marquis stepped nearer to her as he said:

"Then we were both carried away by the drama of what had just occurred, so shall we see today if what we feel is any different, or perhaps even more wonderful?"

As he finished speaking his arms went round her and his lips were on hers.

He held her against him, then he was kissing her not gently or tenderly but demandingly, as if he wanted to be sure of her, as if he wanted to conquer her and possess her completely.

It was like being swept from the despair of thinking she must leave him, into an unbelievably glorious Heaven, and Hermia could only give him her heart and soul as she had given them to him last night.

He kissed her until they were both breathless, until Hermia felt she was no longer herself, but part of him and they were one person.

Then as the Marquis raised his head he said in a voice that sounded strange and a little unsteady:

"You are mine! How could you dare to let another man think you might marry him when you belong to me and have done ever since the first moment I saw you?"

"I . . . I love you!" Hermia said. "I love you . . . until there is no other man in the world but you!"

The Marquis kissed her again.

Now she knew that he wanted to conquer her and dominate her and make her his, so that as she had said there was no other man in the world except him.

Because the sensations he aroused in her were so overwhelming and fantastic, when his lips released her she hid her face against him and he could feel her quivering.

But it was with happiness, not fear.

"What have you done to me, my darling?" he asked.

He laughed.

"I know the answer to that. You have bewitched me and I am in your spell from which I can never escape. I believe now in all the magic with which you have enveloped me from the moment you removed the shoe from my horse's hoof, when I was unable to do so myself."

Hermia gave a little laugh that was almost like a sob.

"It was not magic . . . it was only that being so rich you never have to do such menial tasks for yourself."

"It was magic!" the Marquis averred. "And when I looked at you I thought you had stepped out of a dream."

"You thought I was a milk-maid!"

"I was trying to pretend that you were," he replied, "but I should have realised that you had bewitched me, and I could never escape."

Hermia put her head on his shoulder.

"If I am a witch, I only became one when you kissed me, and I want you to go on kissing me for ever and ever."

The Marquis did not answer.

He merely kissed her and she thought that nothing could be more rapturous, more wonderful than the feelings he evoked in her, or which she realised she was arousing in him.

Only when she could speak did she say:

"I do not believe this is . . . true. I never thought for a moment that you could . . . love me as I . . . love you."

"When you came riding into the wood to perform very badly that piece of play-acting to impress me," the Marquis said, "I knew you were what I had been looking for all my life, and I would never lose you."

Hermia flushed.

"You guessed I was . . . lying?"

"There was no doubt in my mind," the Marquis replied, "even if I had not already been aware that your cousin would no more sit at a dying villager's bedside than carry a wounded man back from a Devil-infested wood!"

"She . . . she is very anxious to . . . marry you."

"I would never have married her!" the Marquis replied. "In fact I had determined never to marry anybody!"

"That is what your sister has told me."

"But, of course, I have no defence against magic."

"You are not to say that," Hermia said quickly. "I could not bear you to think that I tried to catch you or forced you into doing something you did not really wish to do."

The Marquis pulled her against him.

"I am marrying you because I want you," he said, "and I will kill any man who tries to take you away from me."

Hermia thought for a moment, then she said:

"But . . . you brought me to London to . . . meet other men."

The Marquis's arms tightened around her.

"I knew I loved you," he said, "I knew you belonged to me, but I was giving you a sporting chance in case you should prefer somebody else not for your sake, but for mine."

He realised Hermia looked puzzled.

"You see, my darling, having been so disillusioned

I thought all women were the same: ready to sell themselves to the highest bidder, wanting only the position in life I could give them, and not me as a man."

"I want you . . . as you!" Hermia said quickly. "I only wish you were not a Marquis, but just an ordinary man . . . then I could show you how I would look after you and love you."

She moved a little closer to him as she added:

"You would know then that my love is the same that Mama has for Papa and nothing else is of any importance."

The Marquis smiled.

"I realised that when I stayed at the Vicarage," he said. "I have never seen two people as happy as your father and mother, and when I saw how poor you were and how few luxuries you enjoyed, I was almost certain you would feel the same, but I had to be sure."

"But supposing . . . just supposing I had promised to marry Lord Wilchester . . . or somebody like him?"

"Then I should have lost you," the Marquis replied, "because I would have known that to you, thinking I would not marry you, money and position meant more than love."

"And you . . . knew already that I . . . loved you?" Hermia whispered.

"My precious, your eyes are very expressive," the Marquis said, "and I saw when I came into a room how they seemed to light up, and you looked at me in a different way from how you looked at anybody else."

"I . . . I did not realise at first that I . . . loved you,"

Hermia said honestly, "but then I knew it was . . . love which enabled me to find you in the Witch's Cottage, and . . . love which made it possible for me to bring you back to safety."

"And it was love again that made you save me last night," the Marquis added.

"I was so terribly afraid that he would . . . kill you."

"I am alive," the Marquis said, "and now there are no more dangers to threaten us, and only the elves, the fairies and the water-nymphs in which you believe to give us their blessing and to show us how to live happily ever afterwards."

The way he spoke told Hermia he was not laughing at her and she raised her lips to his with a gesture of delight which brought the fire into the Marquis's eyes.

He looked down at her for a long moment before he said:

"I adore you! I love everything about you, your kind, compassionate little heart, the way you think of everybody except yourself, and most of all because you love me! You do love me?"

"I love you until you fill the whole world . . . the sky, the moon and the stars and there is . . . nothing else but you . . . and you . . . and you . . ."

Now there was a note of passion in Hermia's voice that had not been there before and the Marquis's lips sought hers.

He kissed her until she felt as if instead of moonlight there were little flames of fire flickering within her breasts, and he was drawing them up into her lips until they burned against the fire on his.

*   *   *

Some time later Hermia found herself sitting on the sofa, the Marquis's arms around her and her head on his shoulder.

"Now what we have to decide, my precious one," he said, "is how soon we can be married with the least possible fuss."

Hermia gave a little sigh of relief before she said:

"Do you . . . really mean that?"

"I suppose you want a grand wedding," he said, "with all the paraphernalia of bride's-maids and an indefinite number of so-called 'friends'."

"I should hate it!" Hermia said quickly. "I should like to be married very quietly with nobody else there except for Papa, Mama and Peter and because we really love each other, I want no one to snigger or be envious."

The Marquis put his cheek against hers.

"How can you be so perfect? I know of nobody else who would say that to me."

"It is true," Hermia said. "I could not bear to have anybody there hating me or being furious because you had married anybody so insignificant."

She was thinking of Marilyn.

"Then I tell you what we will do," the Marquis said. "We will be married secretly and nobody, except your family, shall know what we have done until we are far away on our honeymoon."

"Do you really mean that?"

"Of course," he replied.

"That would be the most . . . wonderful thing that could ever happen!" Hermia said. "And . . . please . . . can it be very soon?"

The Marquis laughed before he said:

"Tonight, tomorrow or at the very latest two days from now."

Then when Hermia wanted to tell him she was sure it was impossible, she had no chance to do so.

He was kissing her again and his kisses swept her up into a Heaven of happiness where there was only love and him.

*   *   *

The Church had been decorated by her mother with every white flower that the garden possessed.

As Hermia came in through the door on Peter's arm she knew, although the pews were empty, that the whole building was filled with those who had once prayed there, and were now wishing her happiness.

She had not seen the Marquis since she had left London two days earlier with the excuse that because they were all in mourning it was only right for her to return home.

"I am so disappointed, dear child," Lady Langdon said, "but I am sure I can persuade my brother to invite you back again as soon as the summer is over and people return to London for the winter."

She sighed before she continued:

"It will not be as gay as it is now, but there will be Balls and Assemblies, and I should love to chaperon you again."

"You have been very, very kind," Hermia murmured, feeling a little ashamed that Lady Langdon should not know the truth.

But she knew the Marquis was right in saying that if he invited one of his relatives to his wedding the rest would take umbrage for the rest of their lives, and it was therefore best to have all or none.

"The same applies to me," Hermia said. "I am quite sure that Uncle John and Aunt Edith will be absolutely furious, and not only because they were not asked to the wedding."

"Forget what they are feeling," the Marquis said. "I am quite certain your cousin will find an eligible husband sooner or later because she is a very determined young woman."

Hermia did not answer this, as she did not want to seem unkind.

She thought it would be impossible for Marilyn to find anybody as wonderful as the Marquis, and if she had lost him, she knew how miserable she would be feeling.

But it was difficult to think of anything except the happiness of knowing that she would be his wife and they would be together for ever and ever.

"You are quite certain that once you marry me you will not be . . . bored and . . . cynical again?" she asked.

"If as a Witch you cannot prevent me from being bored," he answered, "I shall not think much of your magic."

"Now you are frightening me."

"I love you," he answered. "I love you so much that I know that what we know about each other at the moment is only the tip of the iceberg, and there is so much more for us both to explore and discover which will take at least a century."

Hermia laughed, but she knew it was the truth.

"What is more," the Marquis went on, "I have so much to teach you, my darling one, and love is a very big subject."

The way he spoke made Hermia feel shy, but it

was not the shyness she had felt before.

It was something warm and exciting which seemed to pulsate through her so that she wanted him to kiss her and go on kissing her, and for them to be closer and closer to each other.

"I love you . . . I love . . ." she whispered and then could say no more.

*   *   *

When she returned home and told her father and mother that she was to marry the Marquis, they were at first astounded.

Then when they realised how much she loved him they were happy in a way which made the Vicarage seem to vibrate with joy.

"It is what I have always prayed would happen to you my darling!" Mrs. Brooke said. "I suppose it was foolish of me not to realise that God would answer my prayers, and I should never have doubted for a moment that you would find the same love that your father and I found."

Her mother understood, Hermia thought, as nobody else could have done, how very important it was that her marriage should not be spoilt in any way and must therefore be very secret.

The day after she returned home her wedding-gown arrived from London, and she knew only the Marquis could have chosen something so exquisitely beautiful which was exactly what she would have wished to wear to marry him.

It was white and embroidered all over with tiny diamante which looked like flowers with raindrops on them.

There was a diamond wreath for her hair fashioned in the form of wild flowers that was so beautiful that Hermia thought it must have been made with fairy hands.

When Nanny put the white veil over her face there were tears in the old woman's eyes.

"You don't look real," she said, "and that's the truth! It's just as if you'd come out of the garden or the woods like one of them fanciful creatures you were always talking about when you were a child."

"That is what I hope I look like," Hermia said.

She knew strangely enough it was what the Marquis wanted too, as no other man would have done.

Peter, dressed in the clothes the Marquis had given him, was so pleased with his own appearance that Hermia thought he hardly had time to notice her at all.

"What do you think?" he had said to her when he arrived. "Your Marquis sent a Phaeton and four horses to bring me home, and there was also a letter!"

He drew in his breath as if he could hardly believe what he had read.

"It told me that next term I can have two horses at Oxford of my own, besides a large credit at my new brother-in-law's tailors, which will ensure I can look very nearly as smart as he does!"

"He is so wonderful!" Hermia said softly.

"I think you are wonderful too," Peter said, "and you deserve everything you have and a lot more besides!"

The way he spoke made Hermia smile, and as she walked up the aisle on his arm and saw her father waiting in front of the altar, and her mother sitting in the front pew she thought nobody could be blessed with a more marvellous family.

Then as she saw the Marquis waiting for her she felt as if he was enveloped by a dazzling celestial light.

The angels were singing overhead and the whole Church was filled with the music of love.

*   *   *

After they had cut the cake which Nanny had baked and iced for them and everybody had drunk the excellent champagne the Marquis had brought down with him from London, her father had made a very small speech.

He wished that the happiness they felt at the moment would grow and deepen every year they were together.

Then Hermia had changed into her going-away gown which matched the colour of her eyes and had a light cloak over it, a bonnet trimmed with ribbons and flowers of the same colour.

There were very few people awake in the village as they drove through it. The Marquis had been staying only two miles away and there had been no one to notice his arrival at the Church.

Only as they passed Mrs. Burles's cottage did Hermia see Ben peeping out through one of the windows, and she knew that as usual he would be the first to carry the news around the village that something unusual had occurred.

But now it did not matter.

She was married, she was going away with the man she loved, and the Marquis had already planned a long honeymoon, starting first with a few nights at his country house which Hermia had never seen.

He had already told her that he wanted to show her not only all his treasures inside it, but also the places outside which he had loved as a child.

"The woods meant something to me also," he said, "which I have never confided to anybody except you, and of course, ordinary people would not understand."

"Only witches, fairies and elves!" Hermia smiled.

"And Devils?" he questioned.

"You are not to call yourself that again," she answered. "Now you are back to being the Archangel you were before you fell from grace, and I shall be very angry if anybody calls you a Devil again."

"Except on the race-course," he said, "and my darling, no man in the world could have so much luck as to have you!"

Because it was impossible for Hermia to find words to express how lucky she was she could only press her lips against his.

*　　*　　*

Later that night as Hermia lay in the great State Bed in which the Marquises of Deverille had slept for generations she moved a little closer to the man beside her.

"Are you awake, my precious?" he asked.

"It is impossible to sleep when I am so happy."

His arms held her to him as he said:

"You are quite certain I have not hurt you? You are so precious and so like a flower that I am afraid of spoiling something which is too perfect to be human."

"I adore you," Hermia said, "and when you loved

me it was the most glorious . . . magical thing that ever happened. I felt as if we had wings and flew through the sky towards the . . . moon."

There was a little pause before she said the last word.

Then as she felt the Marquis was curious she explained:

"When I was in London I looked at the moon and felt you were as far out of reach as it was, and that I could never . . . never mean . . . anything to you, except somebody to whom you felt you . . . owed a debt."

The Marquis turned so that he could look down at her.

The only light came from a candle that was beside the bed, but he thought that no one could look lovelier or more ethereal.

"How can I tell you what you mean to me?" he asked, "or explain that you have given me back the dreams, the ambitions and ideals that were mine when I was young?"

"That is what I want you to have," Hermia said. "I could not bear you ever again to be bored or cynical. And, darling, because I love you I feel I have so much to give you."

She knew the Marquis would understand that she was talking about spiritual rather than material things and he said:

"That is what I want to receive and, what we will one day give our children—an understanding of the real value of things, not the tawdry luxuries which can only be counted up in cash."

Hermia gave a little sigh.

"And yet if we spend money in the right way we

can do so much to make people happy. Papa told me last night that he has already started on the Timber-Yard and is employing twenty-five men and hopes to be able to employ more."

She knew that her husband smiled and she went on:

"I also have a suspicion that you and Nanny have come to some special arrangement, which is why Papa and Mama are looking so well. There are a great many delicious things in the larder that I have never seen there before!"

"You should not go poking your nose into other people's business!" the Marquis said.

"I did not believe anybody as . . . important as you could be so human . . . so understanding, so very, very . . . wonderful," Hermia said with a little break in her voice, "and that is why I say you are now an Archangel! And you make me love you more every moment of the day and night."

The Marquis kissed her eyes and said:

"I find you not only irresistible, but an enchantment from which no man could escape."

"Do you . . . want to?"

"You know the answer to that," he said, "and, my precious, how can I ever have thought I was happy before I found you?"

"You did not look happy!"

"I suspected everybody of having ulterior motives, for everything they did and everything they said. Then you came along like a star which had dropped from the sky, and everything changed."

"I want you always to feel like that," Hermia murmured. "But supposing I had lost you?"

181

The horror she had felt when she found him lying on the floor of the Witch's cottage and the memory of his cousin descending from the roof to kill him swept over her.

Instinctively she put out her arms to draw him closer to her as if she would protect him against any danger, any evil.

As if he read her thoughts he said:

"I am safe now and with your love to encircle me, nothing can hurt me. It is love, my precious, that is the magic spell that holds us both enthralled from now until eternity."

"And I love you, my wonderful, kind, marvellous husband," Hermia said, "until there are no words to tell you how much you mean to me."

"I do not need words."

His lips held hers captive, and as she felt his hand touching the softness of her body and his heart beating against hers she knew the fire was rising in him and felt flames flickering within herself.

Then as he carried her up into the sky, they were inside the moon, surrounded by the stars, and there was only love—the love that would hold them spellbound until the end of time.

Barbara Cartland, the world's most famous romantic novelist, who is also an historian, playwright, lecturer, political speaker and television personality, has now written over 370 books and sold over 370 million books the world over.

She has also had many historical works published and has written four autobiographies as well as the biographies of her mother and that of her brother, Ronald Cartland, who was the first Member of Parliament to be killed in the last war. This book has a preface by Sir Winston Churchill and has just been republished with an introduction by Sir Arthur Bryant.

Love at the Helm, a novel written with the help and inspiration of the late Admiral of the

Fleet, the Earl Mountbatten of Burma, is being sold for the Mountbatten Memorial Trust.

Miss Cartland in 1978 sang an Album of Love Songs with the Royal Philharmonic Orchestra.

In 1976 by writing twenty-one books, she broke the world record and has continued for the following six years with twenty-four, twenty, twenty-three, twenty-four, twenty-four, and twenty-five. She is in the *Guinness Book of Records* as the best-selling author in the world.

She is unique in that she was one and two in the Dalton List of Best Sellers, and one week had four books in the top twenty.

In private life Barbara Cartland, who is a Dame of the Order of St. John of Jerusalem, Chairman of the St. John Council in Hertfordshire and Deputy President of the St. John Ambulance Brigade, has also fought for better conditions and salaries for Midwives and Nurses.

Barbara Cartland is deeply interested in Vitamin Therapy and is President of the British National Association for Health. Her book *The Magic of Honey* has sold throughout the world and is translated into many languages. Her designs "Decorating with Love" are being sold all over the U.S.A., and the National Home Fashions League named her in 1981, "Woman of Achievement."

Barbara Cartland's Romances (a book of cartoons) has recently been published in Great Britain and the U.S.A., as well as a cookery book, *The Romance of Food*.